LIONS

Great Days at Grange Hill

'Unless they're real headcases, nobody really likes the idea of starting at their first secondary school . . . the summer holidays drag away as usual – and suddenly there's something chilly in the air. Talk of new uniforms. Talk of PE kit. Moans about how big your feet are getting, how expensive football boots are, embarrassing conferences about whether you'll need to wear a bra or not.'

Judy Preston is scared stiff at the idea of starting her first term at Grange Hill; Trisha Yates is bored stiff. For Michael Doyle it is the start of a long bullying career; and Tucker and his friends are just determined to have a good time, no matter what. And this first term at Grange Hill certainly provides them with all the excitement and tension they could wish for . . .

*Other titles in the Grange Hill series
available in Fontana Lions*

GRANGE HILL RULES O.K.? Robert Leeson
GRANGE HILL GOES WILD Robert Leeson
GRANGE HILL FOR SALE Robert Leeson
GRANGE HILL HOME AND AWAY Robert Leeson
FORTY DAYS OF TUCKER J. Robert Leeson
TUCKER AND CO. Phil Redmond

*Other titles by Jan Needle
available in Fontana Lions*

GOING OUT
MY MATE SHOFIQ
THE SIZE SPIES
ANOTHER FINE MESS
ALBESON AND THE GERMANS
A SENSE OF SHAME AND OTHER STORIES

JAN NEEDLE

Great Days
at Grange Hill

Based on the BBC television series
GRANGE HILL
by Phil Redmond

FONTANA LIONS

First published in Fontana Lions 1984
by William Collins Sons & Co. Ltd
8 Grafton Street, London W1

Copyright © Jan Needle and Phil Redmond 1984

Printed in Great Britain
by William Collins Sons & Co Ltd, Glasgow

For Rod and Julie
and
Chris and Mike

CHAPTER ONE

One Big Happy Family

Unless they're real headcases, nobody really likes the idea of starting at their first secondary school. You finish at primary, the summer holidays drag away as usual – and suddenly there's something chilly in the air. Talk of new uniforms. Talk of PE kit. Moans about how big your feet are getting, how expensive football boots are, embarrassing conferences about whether you'll need to wear a bra or not.

And then it happens. It's the first morning. The alarm has buzzed. Mum has yelled at you, and it hits you like a brick. This is it. The big one. You're not a baby anymore, you're on the verge of growing up. Growing *up*! It's terrifying.

To Judy Preston, huddled under her bedclothes trying still to be asleep, it was like this only worse. Grange Hill High School was looming in her imagination like a monster in a frozen fog, calling her, calling her. And she didn't want to go . . .

To Peter Jenkins, leaning over the bath from his seat on the lav and trying happily to murder a big black hairy spider with his brother's toothbrush, it didn't matter, this Grange Hill dump. He'd pushed it to the back of his mind. For the moment, it did not even exist.

To Benny Green, wandering around in the early morning light, it looked like any other school he'd seen, although bigger than most. It was built of brick, which was one thing, he supposed. It was substantial, not like some of the modern glass and plastic places that looked as if they'd fall down come even a teeny weeny nuclear strike – and the playing fields were more than adequate. Much more. Good, in fact.

Benny, the Brown Bomber, the star footballer of this or any other school (he hoped), bounced his black and white ball a few times and balanced it on his toe as he stared through the fence. Yes, the football facilities looked good. He set off slowly towards the main gate, wondering what time it was. He was early, very early, but he had his trusty ball, which was all that mattered. No point in hanging around the flat.

To Trisha Yates, balancing on her heels and admiring her earrings in the wardrobe mirror, Grange Hill High School was another drag, and another challenge. She felt grown-up already, as grown-up as she ever wanted to be, and this new place just spelled boredom to her – and trouble. She'd seen the circular, she'd had the fights with her Mum and Dad. School uniform was specific, and it got right up Trisha's nose. White socks not tights, no make-up, not even nail polish. And *no* jewellery. It was ridiculous and infuriating. Trisha swept back her long blonde hair with her hand and smiled grimly. She looked as sophisticated as her sister Carol anyway. So just let them try and stop her.

Then the door handle went, and her mother walked in. Trisha spun on her heel, furiously. She had no *right* to do that. Trisha wanted privacy.

In her bed, Judy Preston was fighting a losing battle against the inevitable. Light was pouring through the curtains, and the noise of traffic was building up to its morning crescendo. She felt her stomach, tenderly. Yes, definitely, she was unwell. If she concentrated hard enough she could probably die. She was desperately ill.

Her mother's voice disturbed the sick room. The patient twitched, and did not answer. Her mother had no *feelings*, she didn't *care* that her daughter was suffering. The shout came once more.

'Judy! Are you up yet?'

No reply from the dying girl.

'Judy!' Footsteps on the stairs. The corpse stiffened. 'Judy!'

As the bedroom door opened, Judy Preston let out a groan of despair. Under the covers. She knew she was beaten.

'Oh for goodness sake,' said Mrs Preston irritably, pulling back the curtains. 'Do you know what time it is? *Judy*!'

Of course I know what time it is, thought Judy. You'd be sorry if I did die, I bet. She pulled back the covers and let her hair tumble across her face in an appealing manner. Look of suppressed pain. Agony heroically borne.

'I don't feel well. I've got tummy pains.'

Mrs Preston was too well-bred to snort. But she came close to it.

'Now don't start that again,' she told her daughter briskly. 'You're going to school today and that's that.' She bustled about, getting Judy's things together. Then she smiled, much more gently, which made Judy feel even more forlorn.

'Cheer up,' she said. 'Breakfast's ready. It won't be as bad as all that.'

Judy, who was a timid girl, and shy, and really quite afraid, did *try* to cheer up, without much success, though.

'It will,' she replied. 'Angie Davies said the boys at Grange Hill are horrible.'

'Well you shouldn't listen to what Angie Davies says. And how does *she* know? Has she ever been there?'

That hurt too, because Angie was her friend, and her parents had sent her to a different school, a private school. Grange Hill did have a reputation. Judy sometimes thought her parents should have made the effort as well. They weren't exactly *poor*.

'*Has* she?' insisted Mrs Preston.

'Well. No. But.'

End of friendship, thought Judy. No more good times with Angie.

'Well there you are then. Just think about all the new friends you'll make.'

Mrs Preston started to leave the room. Judy sat on the edge of her bed, feeling desolate.

'But I'm happy with the friends I've got,' she said.

Mrs Jenkins opened the door of the flat to Tucker's mates, Alan Hargreaves and David. They were standing on the landing like a pair of dogs' dinners in their brand new uniforms. She pretended not to know them.

7

'Is Tucker ready yet, Mrs Jenkins?' Alan asked.

'And who might you two posh-looking boys be?'

Alan was shocked. He nearly squeaked.

'It's us, Mrs Jen –' The penny dropped. 'Oh don't you start, Mrs Jenkins,' he begged. 'We've had all that already.'

Tucker appeared behind his Mum, and pushed past. But she caught him on the run. She spun him round and seized his tie. The knot was halfway down his chest.

'Ten minutes you've had it on,' she said, 'and you look a mess already. Peter!'

'I don't like wearing a tie. Why do I have to wear a tie?'

He struggled, but it was no use. She was strangling him. He could feel the knot crushing his Adams apple. Alan and David, loth to see a good man down, moved towards the stairway.

'Now,' said Mrs Jenkins ironically. 'D'you want me to take you to school?'

Tucker gave her one of his looks. By the time she closed the front door the three of them were gone.

In the kitchen of Trisha Yates's house, her fifteen-year-old sister Carol was enjoying the spectacle. Trisha, her face a picture of rebellion, was hopping around with one shoe in her hand. One lumpy, lace-up, sensible leather shoe. One horrible shoe. One hated shoe. Her mother was haranguing her.

'I don't care what you want to wear, Trisha,' she snapped. 'You are not going to school in tights and high heels. Now, put that shoe *on*.'

Carol, looking smart and cool in a dark dress and make-up, smirked elegantly. Trisha would have liked to have spat at her.

'But *Mum*,' she whined. 'Nobody wears these things any more. They're *Stone* Age. Why can't I . . .? *Carol* wears . . .'

Her mother, a plump, easy-going woman, was close to losing her temper.

'Carol is older than you,' she said. 'Carol is in the fifth year and she is *allowed* to by the school. *You* are not Carol.'

'Heaven forbid.' murmured Carol, tossing her dark hair. Trisha hated her.

'But Mum.'

'Trisha! Put . . . them . . . on!'

Her face relaxed as Trisha slowly put on the second shoe. She finally patted her arm.

'You look really good in that uniform, my love,' she said. 'Don't worry. You'll grow up soon enough.'

Sentimental scene. Carol decided to turn the aggro knife. She snatched up her bag and made for the door, fast. She almost got out before Mrs Yates recovered.

'Carol! Where are you going! I told you to wait for Trisha!'

Trisha said sulkily: 'I can go by myself She doesn't have to wait for me. I'd rather go by myself.'

But her mother was getting steamed up again. Her lips grew tight.

'Don't be silly. Carol *wants* to take you. Don't you, Carol?'

'Oh *yeah,*' said Carol, almost out of sight. 'I can't *wait,* can I?'

Mrs Yates looked hard at the door. She touched Trisha's hair.

'You'll like Grange Hill,' she said, in a conciliatory voice. 'Carol likes it.'

'Oh Mum. Don't *fuss.* I'll be all *right.*'

She jerked her head away, which was her last mistake. The earrings were revealed.

'Trisha!' shouted mother. '*No* jewellery!'

Trisha could hear Carol sniggering in the hall. What a way to start a new life . . .

Mr Garfield, the caretaker, watched the school yard and playground filling up with scarcely-concealed gloom. He was beginning to feel he was too old for this game. Just the sight of so many children made him bad-tempered. That little black lad there, for instance. He'd been hanging around the school gates when he'd unlocked them. In the early hours. *Ages* before any kids were normally around. It was a bad sign.

Benny Green, happily unconscious that he was under official scrutiny, continued to kick his ball against the school wall. Sixty one, sixty two, sixty three, sixty four. Mr Garfield began to move towards him, wondering what to bring up first. The lack of uniform, maybe. Jeans were clearly forbidden in the rules. So this boy was probably a trouble-maker. Or perhaps he wasn't even meant to be here. He looked too small to be eleven. An undersized little shrimp. A scruffy, undersized little shrimp.

'You,' he said. 'Don't play ball there, you'll break the windows. Go into the playground.'

Benny trapped the ball expertly. He looked at the bloke in the brown overall coat, recognising the strained look of adult nastiness. He said nothing, and went towards the playground.

Mr Garfield stood still, feeling fed up and crotchety. Children milled around him, teemed all over the place. He watched a big Rover pull up, a gleaming 3.5 litre. A very pale, fragile-looking boy got out and closed the door. He was well turned out, scrubbed-looking, nervous. A cut above the rest of them, thought Mr Garfield. A cut above Grange Hill. If they were *all* like that, if they all came in Rovers and Volvos and Jaguars . . . well, things would be better. The sleek car moved quietly away.

Then the irritation swept back. Pah, thought Mr Garfield. He'll end up a little hooligan, like all the rest of them. His father must be crazy, sending him to a dump like this. Justin Bennett stood there, alone and slightly trembling, clutching his brand new leather briefcase.

The atmosphere in the main assembly hall was subdued. There were about two hundred in the new first year, and most of them were in a similar state to Judy Preston. Her mouth was dry, and she wanted to go to the lavatory. She felt hemmed in, threatened, by the rows and rows of children. The smell of new uniforms was overwhelming, not comfortable and familiar like the smells she remembered from her last school. She was near the back of the

10

hall, but even here there was no rowdyism. Most people were cowed and shaky. Grange Hill, apart from anything else, was enormous.

Tucker Jenkins was neither cowed nor shaky. He was, inevitably, in the very back row, with Alan and David, and they were having fun. Tucker had scored a couple of direct hits with a rubber band and pellets. So far none of the victims who had turned round had managed to spot their tormentor.

The woman who had introduced herself as Mrs Munroe, the head of first year, had finished her speech of welcome and got down to the nitty-gritty. She was going to read out the form numbers, she explained, then the names of the pupils in each form, in alphabetical order. There was a rank of teachers standing by, smiling in that funny way that teachers do when they're trying to show how nice they are really, each one ready to step forward and head a newly formed-up class.

Mrs Munroe smiled a friendly smile, like a nice old auntie.

'When you hear your name,' she said. 'Line up by the door, there. Your tutor will then take you to your form room for registration and time-table. It's really all quite painless. Now. One Alpha.'

One Alpha was Tucker Jenkins's class, if he did but know it. But even if Mrs Munroe had called his name, he would not have heard, naturally. He wasn't listening. As the A's and B's started to pick their way to the waiting form tutor, he was fitting another pellet, taking aim, and letting fly.

Trisha Yates, stung, turned her head quickly. The dark-haired boy with the lively face had done it, obviously. She could tell by the ridiculous look of innocence on his stupid mug. She put on an expression of disgust and turned back to the front. Tucker, Alan and David collapsed in giggles.

'Justin Bennett,' intoned Mrs Munroe. And Justin, licking his lips, crept miserably to the group gathered at the wall.

As Tucker Jenkins drew another bead on Trisha's head, a large hand closed over his. It had come from behind,

11

and it squeezed his painfully. It was a tall, bald teacher, With a very unpleasant expression on his face. Alan and David pretended they weren't with him. Tucker Jenkins quailed.

'Trying to put that young girl's eye out, were you?'

The teacher had a voice like a saw – penetrating and sharp. Even Trisha did not look, because it was so threatening. He held out his hand for the rubber band and Tucker dropped it in. Plus the pellet.

'Were you *born* stupid?' said the voice. It was biting, heavy with sarcasm. Tucker shook his head, staring downwards.

'I see,' went on the voice. 'It's something you've developed yourself, is it?'

Tucker was silent. The teacher rapped the top of his head, hard, with his knuckles. It stung. At the front of the hall Mrs Munroe was saying 'Judy Preston'. And Judy, swallowing drily, moved towards the growing group of new classmates by the wall.

The bald teacher was nearing the end of his routine. 'Don't let me *ever* see you doing that again,' he said. 'Understand? *Do you under stand?*'

Tucker Jenkins nodded, his chin still low on his chest. For a very good reason.

'What's your name?'

'Peter Jenkins, sir.'

The buzz-saw harshened: 'I can't hear you, son.'

Tucker, involuntarily, lifted his head to speak more clearly.

'Peter Jenkins, sir.'

Brief pause. Then, with a note of triumph: 'And where is your *tie* Jenkins?'

'In my pocket, sir.'

Trisha Yates, four feet away, was grinning like a Cheshire cat. She was listening to Mrs Munroe as well, however. She was up to the T's.

Baldie was saying: 'It wasn't designed to go in your pocket, son. It goes around your neck.'

'Yes, sir.'

'Then I suggest you put it on. *Now!*'

Guessing that the teacher was backing off, Trisha Yates, a few seconds later, sneaked a look at Tucker Jenkins. She gave him a dazzling smile.

'Up yours!' it said.

'Ann Wilson,' read Mrs Munroe. Nobody moved. 'Ann Wilson?' Another silence. 'Does anybody *know* Ann Wilson?'

Apparently not. Then it was Trisha's turn. After she had picked up her bag and joined the mob waiting by the wall, she heard Mrs Munroe have one more try. But the mysterious Ann Wilson remained invisible. The head of first year spoke to One Alpha's form tutor, a round-faced man in a sports jacket.

'I'm afraid you appear to be one short, Mr Mitchell. Ann Wilson.'

Mr Mitchell shrugged, and began to marshall the gaggle of kids for the journey to the classroom.

As they left, Mrs Munroe said brightly: 'Good. Now then. One Beta.'

Ann Wilson was on her way. She was almost flying. The alarm clock had not gone off, and she lived quite a way from Grange Hill. When she finally raced into the school grounds, they were deserted. Almost.

A couple of hundred yards away, she could see three girls. They weren't in uniform, and they were pretty smart, so she guessed they must be fifth or sixth formers. The fact that they were late didn't apparently worry them. They were going nowhere fast.

In fact the girls – Jackie Heron, and her sidekicks Brenda and Lucy – were having a quiet bit of fun. They were clustered round a big blackboard standing in a junction of four pathways. It read 'Main assembly hall – this way' and had a white arrow pinned to it. Jackie, a small, plumpish girl with round bright eyes, had just turned the arrow round to point in the opposite direction. They were giggling as Ann Wilson pounded up.

Ann Wilson came from rather a smart estate and she was very confident for her age. She said politely: 'Excuse me. Could you tell me where the main assembly hall is, please?'

Jackie and her mates did not like posh girls. They ate them for breakfast. Jackie sneered: 'Can't you read?'

'Oh,' said Ann, surprised at the unpleasant tone of voice. 'Sorry. But which building is it, please?'

Jackie Heron grinned. And pointed.

'Down there on the right. And it's in front of you. Right?'

Ann smiled. She shook back her long brown hair.

'Thank you,' she said. 'Thank you very much.'

'Don't mention it,' mimicked Jackie. She and her mates wandered off, a job well done.

While Ann Wilson continued searching, Tucker Jenkins mooched moodily down endless corridors with Mrs Munroe, who insisted on calling him Peters. He'd managed to create an authentic problem without trying, for once. At the end of registration, long after he'd seen Alan and David hived off without him, he had realised he was alone. With Mrs Munroe. A touch of panic that he'd failed to catch his own name, then she'd checked her sheaf of papers. Officially, Peter Jenkins (or Jenkin Peters!) did not exist. It was an office job. Come with me, Peters. We'll soon sort you out!

In the doorway of class One Alpha, Mr Mitchell – already dubbed Old Mitch by some of the brighter sparks –was shepherding them in. He had a system, tried and tested over millions of years, which involved them sitting in alphabetical order. Little did he know, thought Trisha, that half of them probably didn't know their alphabet! As Benny Green filed past, Mitchell touched his shoulder. He spoke to him quietly, away from the ruck.

'What's your name, sonny?'

Benny smiled. He liked the look of Mr Mitchell.

'Benny Green, sir.'

'Well, Benny. Don't you know you're only supposed to wear proper trousers to school?'

Benny smiled some more. He'd thought all this out a lot of times, and he was damned if he was going to show embarrassment.

'I haven't got any, sir. My Mum told the headmaster she couldn't afford to buy them, sir.'

Mr Mitchell looked surprised. This boy would never make a politician; too honest!

'Oh,' he said. 'Did she?'

'Yes, sir. My Dad's off work. He fell off a crane and bust his back, sir.'

'Oh. I'm . . . I'm sorry about that, Benny.'

'Oh he's all right, sir. He's going to have to wear a corset like me Mum wears!'

Mr Mitchell almost laughed. I'm going to like you, Benny, he thought.

'Is he?'

'Yeah. It keeps your back straight see, sir. So it won't hurt too much.'

Knockout, thought Old Mitch. He indicated Benny's place among the seated masses. The nervous masses. He spoke to them in a friendly, humorous tone.

'Right,' he said. 'My name is Mitchell and I'm to be your form tutor. The reason you've all been put in alphabetical order is for *my* benefit. As you can see I'm getting terribly old . . .' (Pause for laughter) '. . . and my memory isn't what it used to be. However, the one thing I *can* remember is my alphabet. So hopefully, I'll get to know you all a lot quicker this way, and then you can move about and sit with your friends. Or. . .' (Pause for dramatic effect) '. . . get away from people with smelly socks.'

This time the laughter was less forced, so Mr Mitchell drove the joke home. He went on with a broad grin: 'Or perhaps, those at the front here will want to get away from *my* smelly socks. Anyway . . .' He stopped for some time to let them laugh themselves out. 'Anyway, let's just see if we're all here and make sure no one was kidnapped on the way from the hall. Then we'll see if my terrific system works . . .'

Ann Wilson had one more brush with Heron and her gang before she bumped into Mrs Munroe and Tucker Jenkins. She saw the three fifth formers near a doorway as she trudged embarrassedly across the playground. She ran straight up to them.

'You told me a lie,' she said to Jackie Heron. She knitted her bushy eyebrows into a frown and tried to look fierce. Heron treated her with contempt.

'Are you calling me a liar?'

'Yes,' said Ann. 'You told me –'

She gulped. Jackie Heron was bunching her fists. So were Brenda and Lucy.

'You saw the sign yourself.'

Ann was not going to be intimidated. She didn't frighten easily. But she backed away.

'You probably turned it round or something.'

'So? What are you going to do about it, Mastermind?'

The fifth formers were packing round her closely. Ann felt quite frightened. They *surely* wouldn't . . .?

'Oh look, I'm very late,' she said. 'All I want to do is find the main assembly hall. *Please* tell me where it is.'

Jackie Heron had won. She sneered at Ann and barged her painfully with her shoulder.

'You're so clever,' she said. *'You* find it.'

Well, thought Ann, alone once more. What a charming place I've come to.

Judy Preston and Justin Bennett would have agreed with her. Mr Mitchell had given the class a few minutes chatting time after he'd sorted out the minor chaos they'd turned his system into. Judy and Justin found themselves leaning on a windowsill, side by side, both as miserable as sin.

'Hello,' said Justin, dully.

'Hello.'

'My name's Justin Bennett. What's yours?'

'Judy. Judy Preston.'

They could tell that they were both unhappy. It was *some* sort of bond, at least. After a while, Justin said: 'Is this bigger than your last school? I didn't want to come here.'

'Why not?'

'Because none of my friends are here,' said Justin.

'Neither are mine. My Mum says we'll make lots of new friends, but–'

'*I* won't,' said Justin. 'I *hate* this school.' And before she could agree, Mr Mitchell raised his voice.

'All right, all right you lot,' he shouted. 'Back to your places. And get 'em right this time. Come on, will everybody please sit down.'

Five minutes later, everyone was quietly copying the timetable from the board, with Mr Mitchell answering sporadic questions. In response to one from Benny Green he announced that trials for the football and hockey teams would be held that very week, maybe even next day. Check the notice boards, he went on, or ask –

The door opened and Mrs Munroe appeared with Ann Wilson and Tucker Jenkins in tow. Some of the politer kids stood up. Most did not.

'Sit down please,' said the head of first year. 'Mr Mitchell – I've brought you a couple of waifs and strays. Well, one waif, Peter . . . Jenkins, isn't it . . .' (Tucker smiled; she'd made it!) '. . . and one stray, Ann Wilson.'

'Ah,' said Mr Mitchell. 'Well, we've left a place for you, Ann. Over there. Make yourself comfortable.'

She smiled and set off for the back. Mr Mitchell glanced about. There was a spare desk in front of Trisha Yates.

'Peter,' said Mr Mitchell. 'I wasn't actually expecting you. Er. . . to save disturbing everybody for the moment, you'd better . . . er, just sit over there for now. Right?'

Tucker walked boldly up to the desk in front of the girl with long straight blonde hair and the thin face. He recognised her from the hall. When his back was hiding his hands from Mr Mitchell's view, he flicked her ruler off her desk so that it shot into the air and clattered down. He grinned at her and sat down, eyes front, innocent face. Mrs Munroe moved towards the door.

'Well, there we are, Mr Mitchell. All present and correct. Ready to start their new lives at Grange Hill.'

She beamed at everybody.

'Let's hope,' she said, 'it is a happy experience for them . . .'

Judy and Justin knew it wouldn't be, Ann Wilson thought it would. Benny Green thought of the football trials, Tucker Jenkins wondered how long it was till dinner. Trisha Yates stared at Tucker Jenkin's head, brooding darkly.

Mr Mitchell said heartily: 'Oh, I'm sure it will be, Mrs Munroe. One big happy family!'

As the teachers exchanged confident smiles – hiding who knows what? – Trisha Yates took her first revenge on Tucker Jenkins. The first of many.

She leaned forward and clipped him hard across the head with the sharp side of her ruler. She wished she'd had an axe.

One big happy family . . .

CHAPTER TWO

Benny's Boots

Benny Green was later to school next morning – although he was still well in time – because he'd checked the board the night before. Sure enough, the football trials were scheduled . . . and it had caused him problems. To do the trials, the notice said, you needed proper strip – plus boots. Benny's Mum had done her best, and what strip he did have had been carefully ironed before he left the flat, but it wasn't very good. Basically, since his father's accident – they were skint.

As it happened, Benny almost didn't survive his first five minutes. He entered Grange Hill through the car park gate, and immediately started practising some high toe-kicks with his trusty ball. On the third or fourth bounce he lost control, and ran across the entrance to retrieve it. At the same moment, a small blue sports car buzzed in and missed him by inches. A second later Mr Mitchell stood in front of him, steaming.

'What the *hell* do you think you're doing playing in the car park?' he shouted. 'I could easily have killed you then.'

Benny stared at the ground.

'Sorry, sir,' he mumbled. 'I wasn't looking.'

Mr Mitchell towered over him.

'The cemeteries are full of children who didn't look,' he said.

'But sir –'

Mr Mitchell interrupted him. He was still aerated.

'I know what you were doing,' he snapped. 'You were too damn involved with that football.'

He stared at Benny and Benny stared at the ground. What else was there to do? Mr Mitchell sighed.

'Go and get it,' he said. The anger had left his voice. Benny Green stepped guiltily onto a flower bed and got his ball back. He returned to the form tutor.

'Benny Green, isn't it?' The voice was calm. Quite kind.

'Yes sir.'

Mr Mitchell was trying to be nice now. Benny was grateful.

'Did you play for your last school team? Our trials are tonight, you know. Got your kit?'

Benny indicated the scruffy duffel bag sagging from his shoulder.

'PE kit, sir.'

'Well – got your boots?'

Benny looked briefly into Mr Mitchell's face. He'd sworn never to be embarrased about his family's poverty – and anyway, he thought this guy would understand.

'No,' he said. 'The ones I had got too small and my Dad gave them to my little brother, sir.'

Mr Mitchell made a face.

'Well,' he said. 'I don't think you'll be allowed to –' He observed Benny's expression, and made his voice brighter. 'Still. We'll see.' He made a gesture. 'Go on,' he said.

Benny mooched off, feeling glum. He heard the sports car moving off behind him. If he couldn't get a trial, he thought, he might just as well have been run over . . .

As soon as Tucker Jenkins entered the gate he saw Alan and David ahead of him. Only the second day and already the pillocks hadn't bothered to call for him, just because they were in different classes! He changed down a gear and powered towards them. At the last second he rose from the ground on full blast-off and flew towards their unsuspecting necks.

'Banzai!'

He crashed into them, and all three fell in a heap. Arms, legs, schoolbags, football boots, kit. Amid laughter and swearwords they began to pick themselves up out of the ruck.

A hand thrust its way into the jumble and seized Jenkins by the front of his shirt. A big hand. An adult hand. A man's hand.

'Fancy yourself as something of a circus performer do you, son? A bit of a clown are you?'

20

It was the grating tones of the teacher in the hall. The bald one. Oh God, thought Tucker. If he recognises me!

The man – Mr Foster in public, Frosty when he wasn't there to hear it – let go of Tucker's neck. Tucker kept his eyes well down.

'What would your mother say,' rasped Mr Foster, 'if she saw you rolling about in that new uniform?'

'Don't know sir.'

'Look at me when I'm talking to you, son.' Tucker half looked up. 'What's your name?'

Out of the corner of his eye, Tucker saw David smirking. Blond-haired twit. You could go off people, you know. But the monster was waiting for an answer.

'Er,' he went. 'Er . . .'

'Well come on. I take it you can remember your own name.'

I can, thought Tucker. It's *you* I'm worried about!

'Jenkins, sir.'

Mr Foster stood rigid, trying to remember. Tucker Jenkins offered up a small prayer to whoever might be listening. I'll be a better person, he lied.

'Jenkins,' mused the master. 'I know you, don't I?'

Alan and David began to shuffle, nervously.

'Don't think so, sir.'

'Didn't I have cause to speak to you yesterday? In the hall? About firing paper pellets?'

Tucker Jenkins was a picture of wounded innocence.

'No sir,' he said. 'Not *me*, sir.'

Mr Foster was suspicious, but he wasn't sure. So many new kids, so many. His voice became more cutting yet.

'Don't mess me about, laddie,' he said. 'Because it doesn't pay.'

'I wasn't sir. It wasn't me, sir.'

'Hhm.' Mr Foster capitulated. 'Well, I'll be watching out for you, Jenkins. Remember that. Just don't let me catch you playing the buffoon again. Got it?'

Tucker gave a humble nod, and the three of them shuffled off.

'Phew,' said David, when they were out of earshot. 'You took a chance there, Tucker.'

'Dah!' said Tucker. 'I knew he'd never recognise me. And the size of this place, I'll probably never see him again!'

Grange Hill was big all right. After registration, for instance, Benny Green got lost for ages, trying to find the changing rooms. But if Tucker thought he could keep away from the thin-faced teacher with the bald bonce, he had two thinks coming and a bonus. Mr Foster was taking them for games.

Tucker arrived at the changing rooms later than most – except Benny – but he went straight to the head of the queue. Justin Bennett was standing there, reminding Tucker very much of a rather wet-looking girl. He had a thin, serious face, and straight black hair, quite long. He was incredibly pale, although he didn't appear to be dying of some dreadful disease.

'Is this changing room three?' asked Tucker. 'Are you in One Alpha?'

'Yes.'

Tucker dropped his bag.

'Thank *Gawd* for that. I've been looking for ages. This place is too big. Do we have to go in and change or something?'

Justin shook his head.

'I don't know. I expect we have to wait for the PE tutor. Everybody else is. I think it's too big, too. It's much bigger than my other school.'

Tucker looked at Justin curiously. He sounded quite aggrieved, as if the size of the school was a personal insult.

'Don't you like it, then?' he asked.

'No,' said Justin, flatly. 'I hate it. I absolutely hate it.'

Blimey, thought Tucker. You are a bit wet, sunshine. Then he heard the voice. The dreaded chainsaw.

'And exactly *what* are you doing standing here?'

Mr Foster, when he'd told them off for not being ready, and stormed them into the changing room, went on at great length. He did not exactly introduce himself as a swine, but he wasn't far off. He made everything sound extremely unpleasant, and he made it clear to even the

22

dimmest that they were not going to do anything silly like actually enjoy games. The elements of nastiness were introduced as 'simple rules' of course, which would make things 'better for everybody'. To rub them in he twisted ears and pulled hair for fun. Welcome to the Scrubs!

'Right,' the man said. 'I would now like to remind you that adequate, proper and *decent* strip will be worn at all times.' He pulled out a boy who was ready and twirled him round in front of the others. 'That means – *vest, shorts, footwear.*' The boy was pushed back to his bench. 'And with regard to footwear, gentlemen. It *must* be worn. Bare feet will not be tolerated. *Neither* will anything other than proper gym shoes. Black-soled shoes are not, repeat *not,* allowed in the gymnasium. Nor are football boots, spiked running shoes, hob-nailed boots, beetle crushers, desert wellies or whatever. Do I make myself absolutely clear?'

They were getting the message. The answer rang out clearly: '*Yes* sir.'

'Splendid,' rasped Mr Foster. 'Three basic rules, that's all. One. Be ready when I arrive. Two. Only do what you are told inside gymnasium. And three –' He stabbed a finger at Justin Bennett.

'Er. I. Er.'

'Next lad! Number three?'

'Proper kit, sir!'

'Which is? Next lad!'

'Vest, shorts and pumps, sir!'

'Yes!' said Mr Foster. 'Or more correctly, *clean* vest, shorts and shoes.' He moved down the line and stopped in front of Tucker.

'Well well. If it isn't Mr Jenkins. If it isn't the intrepid circus performer.' He flicked at the rolled-up sleeve of his vest. It was rolled because Tucker thought it looked hard, and the kit was crumpled because he'd screwed it up in his bag. His mother would have killed him. Maybe Foster would, instead.

But Foster only grated out: 'What's this?'

'My kit, sir. It's clean, sir.'

The sarcasm was amazing.

'Perhaps it is, Jenkins. But you look more like a discarded fish and chip paper than a potential athlete, son. Don't you?'

The class giggled. It was safest, when a teacher made a joke. And nice, to see someone else collecting all the flak. Jenkins made a private face. Prat, he thought.

'A slovenly appearance, gentlemen, is the result of a slovenly character,' said Mr Foster. 'My gymnasium was never intended to be, is not, and never will be a sanctuary for slovenly characters, rag-bags, or apprentice scarecrows. Is that clear, Jenkins?'

Tucker said through gritted teeth: 'Yes, sir.'

'Splendid. Right. First boy. Lead out!'

Benny Green finally made it into the gym about five minutes later, and feeling a total fool. After blundering around the school for ages and at last getting directions from an older boy, he had gone into a deserted changing room and started to strip off hurriedly. When he was down to a pair of snazzy underpants and his medallion, the door had opened and a woman PE teacher had come in. Followed by a gang of females. It was the girls' side. Benny, covered in confusion and a towel, had scuttled off amid screams of girlish laughter.

As he pushed open the door of the gym, Mr Foster was having some fun at Tucker's expense.

'This,' he said, picking one from off the floor, 'is a medicine ball. We use it to develop and strengthen the stomach muscles, like so. Catch!'

The heavy leather ball caught Tucker in the stomach, and he fell. Mr Foster smiled.

'You disappoint me, Jenkins,' he said. 'I would have thought a man of your acrobatic prowess would have been able to . . .'

He stopped in mid-sentence as Benny let the door swing to. He watched as Benny, happy at last, strode briskly up to the circle of boys, his arms swinging smartly. He composed his face as Benny stopped.

'And just who might you be?'

'Green, sir,' replied Benny with a half-smile. 'Sorry I'm late. I got lost in the changing rooms.'

'*Did* you? And exactly where do you think you are going now?'

Benny was puzzled.

'To join the class, sir.'

Foster's eyes travelled up and down him. From his bare feet, to his bare chest. Benny Green was wearing only shorts. And his medallion.

'Oh no you are not, son. Not dressed like that you are not. You are going back to the dressing room. No strip. No lesson.'

'But I haven't got one, sir.'

'Your parents were issued with a circular, I take it? Regarding appropriate PE strip?'

Benny did not let his eyes drop.

'Yes, sir,' he said. 'But my Mum couldn't afford one.'

There was an uneasy stirring in the group. Everyone thought Foster was being horrible. Foster was unmoved.

'Then borrow one, lad,' he said.

Benny was amazed.

'Where from, sir?'

A small smile appeared on the teacher's face.

'That,' he said, 'is your problem. Use your initiative.'

Benny stood his ground for two more seconds, then gave it up. As he turned for the door Mr Foster picked up a medicine ball and threw it at a boy.

'Return,' he said, then threw it to the next.

Benny, apparently forgotten, left the gym. He put his clothes back on and sat in the changing room, alone. Bad, he thought. Bad, bad, bad.

There was worse to come from Frosty Foster. At the end of the lesson he reminded the class about the football trials. They were at 4.30 – 5 o'clock kick-off – after the girls' hockey trials. It was all bundled together somewhat because of drainage work on some of the pitches. Benny, trying to get some information and also show himself to be polite and reasonable as well asked a question.

'Please, sir. How do we enter for the trials?'

Foster eyed him up and down.

'Just report here with your strip at 4.30 precisely. And Green. I mean a *proper* and *adequate* football strip. *Not just shorts.*'

Benny remained polite, although he felt like murder.

'I could play in my shirt and shoes, sir.'

'Rubbish,' said Foster. 'I'm not having your mother coming here complaining about you ruining your clothes, son. Adequate strip – or nothing.'

As he stalked out, Tucker Jenkins barged in front of Benny and did an ape performance towards the door Frosty had gone through. The two of them walked back to the benches together.

'Are you going in for the trials?' asked Benny. He sounded dejected.

'Dead right,' replied Tucker Jenkins. 'You?'

'You heard what he said,' said Benny. 'I haven't got a kit.'

'Why don't you borrow one?'

'Where from?' asked Benny.

Tucker did a lousy imitation of the teacher's voice.

'That,' he rasped, 'is your problem, son. Use your initiative!'

Benny managed a little laugh, although he felt far from being jolly. But Tucker had bounced to his feet. He walked round the bench and confronted Justin Bennett.

'Hey. You going in for the trials tonight?'

'No,' said Justin. 'Why?'

'You won't be needing this then, will you!'

He picked up Justin's sports vest.

'Hey! Give it back!'

Tucker returned to Benny, with Justin following. Justin didn't dare try and grab it, but he tried to sound tough.

'Give that back,' he repeated.

'Oh go on,' said Tucker. 'Lend it to him. You'll get it back tomorrow.'

'I don't see why I should lend it to you,' said Justin, nervously. Tucker laughed.

'Not lending it to me, are you? You're lending it to him. It'll come back washed, won't it?'

Benny nodded.

'That's settled then,' said Tucker. He held it out to Benny. 'There you are, sir. One sports vest. Only one previous owner. A bit sweaty, but otherwise guaranteed.'

Benny looked at Justin. They were both nonplussed.

'Thanks,' he said. And Justin walked away.

'Well,' said Tucker. 'All you need now is a pair of boots and socks.'

He winked at Benny. It would be a pleasure to do this Foster swine down, a real pleasure. And he thought he might have made a mate, into the bargain. Benny Green and Tucker Jenkins left the changing rooms together.

Tucker wasn't all that bright over some things, and Benny's heart sank when he saw the mate he'd brought along to lend him his boots. He was waiting on a stairway outside the main building, overlooking the playing fields, when Tucker came panting around the corner.

'Ah,' said Tucker. 'There you are. This is my mate, Alan. He stinks a bit, but he's OK really. He won't be doing the trial but he's doing games today so he's got his boots.'

Alan smiled.

'You can borrow them if they fit.'

Not much chance though. Alan was about a foot taller than Benny, and fat with it. It turned out the boots were three times bigger than his feet. Useless.

When Alan had gone, Mr Mitchell came through the door onto the staircase. He noticed Benny's face.

'What are you two plotting, then?'

'Nothing, sir.'

'It's Benny, sir,' said Tucker. 'He wants to play in the football trials, but Mr Foster won't let him because he's got no boots.'

Mr Mitchell frowned.

'Have you tried to borrow a pair?'

'Yes sir,' Benny replied. 'My feet are too little.'

'Oh,' said Mr Mitchell. 'It's not your lucky day, is it, Benny?' He did not wait for an answer. He looked at his watch.

'Look,' he said. 'It's almost time for registration. You'd

better get along to the classroom. Something might turn up.'

'Yeah,' Jenkins muttered. 'Mr Foster might break his neck in the –'

'Jenkins! Now, get along to the classroom. I'll be with you shortly.'

When Mr Mitchell entered One Alpha some minutes later and quietened them down, he did not tell them why he was late. What was the point, he thought. A total waste of time. At times Tony Mitchell despaired of some of his colleagues, and now was one of them.

He'd arrived at the gym to find Mr Foster hanging upside down from a pair of ropes. Jenkins's comment about broken necks flashed through his mind, but he suppressed a smile. He got on Foster's right side by not walking in with his outdoor shoes on, but it did not help. He tried the lot – reason, soft soap, the little lad's terrific record as a footballer at his last school, the effort he'd made to get the kit together. To no avail.

'I'd like to help,' rasped Mr Foster, 'but you know my rule, Tony. If I let one get away with it – especially at the beginning of term . . . You know my rule.'

'Yes,' said Mr Mitchell. 'No exceptions.'

'No exceptions,' repeated Foster. 'Sorry, Tony.'

'Yes,' said Mr. Mitchell. 'Well thanks, Dan. Thanks anyway.'

For nothing.

Now the class was watching him, attentively. All but Trisha Yates, who was sitting in the front row reading a magazine. As he came close she noticed him and slipped it into her desk. Then retrieved it and put it into his hand. It was a glossy. Called *Passion*.

'Yes,' said Mr Mitchell. 'Very good, Trisha. But I think passion can wait till four o'clock!'

When the laughter had died down, he told the class formally about Benny's boots, or lack of them. They had not been a class for very long, he said, but he hoped they might want to help. The trouble was – they only had the afternoon to do it in. Any suggestions?

Hughes, who was something of a comic, weighed in. He

said they should ask his family's dog, who was very keen on sports.

'Is he, Hughes?' asked Mr Mitchell, playing along. 'And why is that?'

Hughes almost bust a gut.

'Because he's a boxer, sir!'

Ho ho ho, very funny, went the class.

Margaret Shaw, at the back, thought her brother's feet were as diddy as Green's, but admitted she couldn't get home and back in time. Stalemate.

Then Ann Wilson, inevitably, had a brainwave. Benny Green took size threes, she took size threes. She was having a hockey trial, *before* the football trial. And hockey boots were a *bit* like soccer boots, weren't they?

'Yeah,' said Tucker sarcastically. 'Just like my grandad used to wear.'

But it was agreed. Benny tried them on – a shade reluctantly – and they were a reasonable fit. Mr Mitchell beamed. Then spoiled it all by making them get their books out – and do some rotten work!

The problem was, that at half past four, when everyone had to be kitted up and ready in the changing rooms, Ann Wilson still had not turned up. Tucker barged in just in front of Frosty Foster and sat with his back to Benny, at the end of a double-row of benches. He whispered the bad news, then his plan. As Foster started his slow inspection walk, Benny agreed to give it a whirl.

It worked like this. When Foster had stared at Jenkins – shirt, shorts, socks, boots – he nodded and walked on. He had to work his way right up one row, round the end, and back down the other side. By the time he arrived at Benny's place Tucker had slipped off his boots, passed them behind him to his mate, and Benny was tying up the laces. All Foster could do was look meaningfully at his watch and make noises. But he was beaten. Benny was kitted out.

'Right,' said Foster. 'Outside in five minutes.'

'Give me the boots,' said Tucker, when he'd gone. 'Hide in the shower in case he comes back. I'll go and see if I can find that girl again.'

So desperate was he, after a couple of minutes' wait, that he opened the door to changing room two – the girls' room. And got a flea in his ear from a PE mistress. When he dared peep out of the boys' side again, he saw Ann Wilson racing up.

'About time too,' he snapped. 'Where have *you* been!'

Ann was very refined. She refrained from clouting him.

'I had to finish my game, you know. And I had to run from –'

'All right, all right! Just give me the boots. I'm late enough as it is.'

He dashed off, leaving Ann outside the changing room in her socks.

'*Thank* you, Ann,' she said, to thin air. 'Oh! Don't mention it . . .'

Two minutes later Tucker dashed out of the boys' room, almost knocking Mr Mitchell over on the way. The form master went across to Benny.

'Come on, Green,' he said, good-temperedly. 'We're all waiting for you. I just hope after all this that Mr Foster's satisfied.'

'So do I,' said Benny Green. He meant it.

Outside, as Tucker raced onto the field, Foster said impatiently: 'Come along, come along. Is there anybody else?'

'Benny's just coming, sir,' panted Tucker Jenkins. 'He won't be a second.'

'I should think –'

Mr Foster stopped. Benny was walking onto the pitch, with Mr Mitchell beside him. He ran the last few yards – with Mr Foster's beady eyes fastened on the boots. Black canvas, with rubber soles.

'Just a minute, son,' he said. He gripped Benny by the ear, hard. 'Are those hockey boots you're wearing?'

'Er. Yes, sir,' said Benny Green.

Mr Foster's eyes narrowed. He smelled a rat. He let go of Benny as Mr Mitchell strolled up.

'How did you get past my inspection?'

'Er. I . . . I . . .' Benny Green looked into the face of his form tutor. Mr Mitchell smiled. At Dan Foster.

'You used your initiative, didn't you, Green?' he said.

He raised his eyebrows ironically. Everybody waited, silent.

And Mr Foster, rather sourly, accepted defeat.

'Odd ones that end, even this,' he said.

He raised the whistle to his lips, and blew.

The trial was under way.

CHAPTER THREE

Enemies . . . And Friends

Although Judy Preston hadn't bothered with the symptoms of terminal illness since the first morning at Grange Hill, she'd tried in various subtle ways to let her mother know just how much she hated the place. The trouble was – as her mother did not tire of telling her – she was a busy woman, and her father was a busy man. That's how they managed to have a bit of money around, and that's why Judy was such a lucky girl. Circular argument. Simplicity itself. But I'm *not* lucky, Judy told herself. Why couldn't *they* see that?

She sat on the sofa, morosely finishing her cup of coffee, looking like everybody's idea of the perfect schoolgirl. Smart uniform, pressed skirt, tie neatly tied. Scrubbed pink face, newly washed hair, long, blonde and shiny, with crinkly ends. And she was as miserable as anything.

As her mother bustled about the lounge, Judy went to the mirror in front of the gas fire and started to brush her hair. It didn't need it, but it was something to do. The static electricity crackled in the brush with the force of the strokes. Her mother called to her.

'Come on Judy, you're going to be late again. Judy! Hurry up!'

Judy ignored her and went on brushing. Mrs Preston, getting her things together, noticed what she was doing.

'Judy! How many times have I told you not to brush your hair in front of the fire. It's dangerous!'

She dragged her daughter unceremoniously away from the fire and turned it off. She grabbed her shoulder and made a few vigorous strokes with the brush herself. Judy felt full of spite.

'Well you shouldn't have put the mirror *there*,' she snapped.

Mrs Preston kept her cool.

'Yes. Well,' she said. 'You use the one outside in future.' She put the brush down. 'There. Now go and get your coat.'

As she turned away, Judy picked up the brush once more. After a few more dabs she moved to the coffee table and started flicking through a magazine. Mrs Preston, getting her coat on, shouted: 'Judy! What *are* you doing?'

'I'm *looking* for something.'

Patience on a monument. 'I can see that but . . .' Patience falling off a monument. 'Now *really*, Judy, I shouldn't have to chase you off to school every day.'

Judy matched irritation with irritation. 'I don't *like* it at Grange Hill.'

Mrs Preston turned her eyes to heaven.

'Oh come on, let's not start all that again. You've only been there a few days.'

Judy said sulkily: 'It's too big. No one ever speaks to you, and you're always left on your own.'

Mrs Preston was getting furious.

'Well. Do you ever speak to them?' Judy's expression was the answer. 'Well. There you are then, Judy. You really must make the effort to . . .' Her daughter's face got even more unhappy. Mrs Preston softened. 'Oh look, I'll tell you what we'll do. I haven't got time to talk about it now but we'll sit down and we'll discuss the whole thing tonight. OK?'

Judy, unfortunately, had heard it all before. But her parents were *always* too busy.

'You always say that,' she said. 'But we never do.'

'Well we will tonight, I promise.' Big smile.

'You always say *that*, too.'

Mrs Preston snapped.

'Oh look, Judy! *I've* got to get to work as well, you know! We'll talk about it tonight! We will!'

A pause. I've done it now, she thought.

'Oh here,' she said, fumbling in her handbag. 'Here's twenty pence. Buy yourself something to cheer you up on the way. Go on.' Another big smile. 'There. Now get your coat on.'

Judy took the money, avoiding her mother's eyes. Great, she thought. The answer to everything. Twenty pee's worth of instant happiness. Ho. Ho. Ho.

The rest of form One Alpha was already assembled when Judy arrived. They were sitting at their desks in reasonable array, except for Tucker Jenkins and Benny Green, who were heading Benny's plastic ball across the rows at each other. As Judy walked past, Tucker bounced it hard off the back of her head.

As Judy spun round, Benny grabbed her bag, darted down the class, and tossed it over her head to Tucker. He shot it back, and as Judy lunged for it, Benny whooshed it over her head to his mate. The classroom collapsed into roars of approval, mixed with shouts of 'Leave her alone' from a couple of girls.

Judy was beginning to get upset when Trisha Yates intervened. She moved smartly out of her place as the bag flew from Benny to Tucker, and reached up a hand to catch it. With the other, she caught Tucker off balance very skilfully, and knocked him sprawling. Amid howls of derision and a few cheers, she handed the bag to Judy. She was a mean fighter, was Trisha.

Tucker scrambled to his feet and confronted her.

'What did you do that for?' he demanded belligerently.

'Because I felt like it.'

'It was none of your business.' Tucker put his face close to Trisha's but she didn't move a muscle. She was slightly bigger than him.

'I made it my business.'

Hmm. Tucker almost backtracked.

'We were only playing piggy in the middle.'

She smiled.

'You should have been in the middle then, shouldn't you?'

There was a roar of laughter from the audience. Tucker was definitely coming off second best.

'Do you want me to thump you?' he said, making a fist.

Trisha Yates pushed her face into his.

'Yeah? You and whose army?'

'Yah,' said Tucker, feeling a right twit. 'I don't fight with girls. You're not worth fighting anyway.' He set out for his desk.

He'd had his nose put out, for sure. Trisha grinned nastily at his retreating back. She walked to Judy's desk.

'Don't let him worry you,' she said. 'He's all talk. Your name's Judy Preston isn't it? I'm Trisha Yates. See you later.'

Suddenly, Judy started feeling good. Daft, maybe, but this looked like the start of something. She smiled foolishly at Trisha Yates's back. And composed herself as Mr Mitchell came in.

'Good morning, everybody,' he said, in his funny, jokey way. He wiggled his eyebrows as a few of them answered him.

'I see you're settling in then,' he went on. 'You've learnt the first rule – ignore the staff!'

There were some giggles.

'And why not indeed?' said Mr Mitchell. 'I do it all the time!'

When they'd settled down, he called on Benny Green to stand.

'Now, Mr Green,' he said. 'Mr Foster –'

Tucker Jenkins made a rude noise. Mr Mitchell paused, then soldiered on.

'Mr Foster has asked me to inform you that you have been selected for the school team on Saturday. There's one condition, though. You need a pair of proper boots.'

Benny smiled happily. Great news!

'That's all right, sir,' he said. 'My mum had a bingo win. She said she'd get me a pair. And a strip. If I made the team. And I . . .'

'And you did,' said Mr Mitchell. 'Congratulations.'

'What about me, sir?' said Jenkins, cheekily. 'Have I been picked?'

'Jenkins,' said Mr Mitchell, 'considering what a stickler for discipline our Mr Foster is – I doubt if he'd pick you if you were a spot. But I only have inside information on Mr Green in any case. Watch the notice board.'

Tucker, lost once more in hoots of laughter, decided to keep his mouth shut for a while. He kept putting his foot in it . . .'

Judy Preston was full of hope as the class streamed into the playground. She stopped at a corner of the wall near the entrance door, and held her breath as Trisha and another girl approached. 'I'll see you later,' Trisha Yates had said.

Much later, obviously. For Trisha did not even notice her, pressed against the wall with a friendly, foolish grin on her face. Stupid, stupid, stupid, Judy cursed herself, as the girls walked past in conversation. Stupid to think anyone could care. Stupid to think anyone would like her. She felt like crying.

Somebody had noticed Judy Preston though – and was smart enough to recognize the symptoms. Of a lonely, friendless . . . victim. Jackie Heron nudged her mates.

'Look, Brenda,' she said. 'Over there. Come on, Lucy.'

They were experts at cornering and bullying, and before she even knew it, Judy was surrounded. She felt a rush of fear as they pressed up to her, big girls, grown-up girls, who weren't in uniform. Jackie Heron pushed her shoulder and Brenda, on her left, dug her in the stomach.

At that moment, luckily, a master appeared and walked towards them. Heron and her sidekicks eased back for a moment, looking casual. Judy took her chance. She slipped between two of the bully-girls and fled. They noted carefully which entrance she ran through into the building.

Inside, Judy rushed down a corridor a short way, then slowed down. She didn't want to be in trouble with the teachers as well. She stared through a wire-netted window to see if the big girls were after her. Nothing. She thought she might go home. Run away from this dreadful school. She went into the cloakroom and found her coat. She couldn't really, though. What would her mother say?

Too late she realized she was trapped. As Jackie Heron's face appeared between two coats, Judy turned and ran down the line of pegs. Into the arms of Brenda and Lucy, who seized her roughly and marched her backwards to their leader.

'It isn't polite to run away when someone wants to talk to you,' said Jackie Heron, almost pleasantly. 'Is it, girls?'

They grinned. Brenda opened her mouth and a pale pink sheet of bubble gum emerged and disappeared.

'What's your name?'

'Judy,' she whispered. 'Judy Preston.'

'Judy, eh.' Jackie Heron bunched her fist and brandished it. 'How about a *punch*, then?'

Judy was terrified, and it showed. Jackie Heron smiled sweetly and dropped her fist.

'It's my birthday today,' she said. 'Did you buy me a present?'

Judy shook her head, bewildered.

'Oh never mind. I'll forgive you. Perhaps you'd like to give me something so that I can buy a present for myself?' No response. 'Brenda!'

Brenda took a large handful of Judy's hair and tugged. Jackie Heron said: 'Well?'

'Oh please . . . please leave me alone.'

'Lucy!'

Lucy went into the next part of the well-rehearsed routine. Fast and expertly, she went through Judy's blazer pockets, throwing pencils, hairgrips, a letter, onto the floor. She gave the purse to Jackie Heron, who snapped it open. The 20p – unspent on principle – shone in her hand.

'Only twenty pence,' she said, disgustedly. 'Your parents are a bit stingy, aren't they? That won't even buy me a birthday card.'

Lucy, who had just been through the blazer's inside pocket, handed her a fountain pen. Judy squeaked in horror.

Heron said: 'I like this pen, though. That would make a *lovely* birthday present.'

'Oh *please*. Please don't take that. My grandad bought me – ooooow!'

Brenda only stopped pulling when Judy was on the edge of tears.

'So,' said Jackie Heron. 'Grandpapa bought it, did he? Snuffed it, has he? I bet it's worth something to you, then. Sentimental value and all that rubbish. I'll tell you what I'll do. Seeing as I like your face.'

Brenda laughed and blew another bubble. Jackie Heron carried on.

'I'll give you the chance to buy it back, Judy. Does fifty pence suit you?'

Judy had to nod, because Brenda almost had her hair out by the roots. She nodded.

'In that case,' smirked Heron. 'I'll make it seventy. Nod if you agree.'

Nod nod nod.

'Good. We'll see you later then.'

The three girls disentangled themselves and moved off a foot or so. Jackie's eyes were full of menace.

'Oh,' she said. 'And don't get any ideas about telling the staff. Understand?' Her face relaxed. 'Good. Bye now!' It sounded almost pleasant.

In the corridor, the three girls walked past Trisha Yates. She was moving slowly, because she had a splinter in her hand. She paused by the cloakroom window to poke at it, and caught a movement in the corner of her eye. She squinted into the dim, long room and saw Judy on her hands and knees. Trisha went in.

'Judy! What's up? What's been happening?'

Judy, almost crying, could not explain.

'Nothing!'

'Is it that Peter Jenkins? Has he been bothering you again? What's –'

'Nothing!' Judy picked up the last of her things and started to barge out. 'Leave me *alone!*'

Trisha pulled a face. What a funny girl, she thought. No wonder no one spoke to her . . .

Trisha Yates and Carol never had a lot to say to each other – not a lot that was printable, anyway – but Trisha was even quieter than normal as they walked home at dinnertime. She was still thinking about Judy Preston and the scene in the cloakroom. And not making a lot of sense out of it. If she'd had X-ray vision, though, she'd have known she was about to see the quiet girl again. Soon.

Judy Preston had been walking along a couple of hundred yards in front of Trisha and her sister – also deep in thought. So much so, that she had not noticed Jackie Heron and her friends, outside a tobacconists, opposite the common. As she passed the open space outside the shop, she was dragged off the pavement and slammed against an advert hoarding.

'Hello, Judy,' said Jackie Heron, in mock surprise. 'Fancy meeting *you* here! You haven't forgotten it's my birthday, have you?'

'Let me go! Let me go! You're hurting me!'

'Oh I *am* sorry,' smiled Jackie Heron. 'But don't you *want* grandpapa's pen back?'

'Of *course* I do,' said Judy. 'But I haven't got any *money*.'

'Then *get* some.'

'Where *from*?'

The girls made noises with their mouths. Don't be so stupid noises. Heron shook her head in disbelief.

'You're going home for lunch, aren't you? Where do you live?' A jerk on Judy's hair. '*Where do you live*!'

Judy said quietly: 'Rockfield estate.'

'*Do* you now! Then your parents must be worth a bit! Ask Mummy. She'll give it to you, won't she?'

Judy bit her lip.

'What happens if she won't?' she asked.

'Simple, Judy. It's goodbye to grandpapa's pen. Got it?'

It was at this point that Trisha, passing on the other side of the road with Carol, spotted the group of girls. She stopped, puzzled.

'That's strange,' she said.

'What is?' said her sister. 'Come on, let's get home. What are you gawping at?'

'That girl's in my class. The one with long blonde hair.'

'So?'

'She's not got any friends. She never speaks to nobody.'

Carol glanced across the road. Her expression altered.

'It doesn't look that way to me,' she said. 'And if I was her I wouldn't have *that* lot for friends.'

'Why? What's wrong with them?'

'Everything. Just keep away from them. And tell your friend the same.'

She turned and struck out across the common. Trisha waited for a second more.

'Are you coming?' Carol called. 'Or are you going to stand round catching flies all day?'

Trisha closed her mouth and followed.

Trisha bolted down her dinner, and kept dropping broad hints for Carol to hurry up. Carol took her time, naturally, and would not speed up on the walk back to Grange Hill. When they got to the spot opposite the newagents, though, it was Trisha who slowed down. She was not entirely surprised to see that Jackie Heron and her mates were still hanging around. They also appeared to have another victim, a little kid of eight or so. She stopped to watch.

'What's up now?' said Carol.

'Er. I think I'll nip across and buy something,' said Trisha. 'Hang on a sec.'

She slowed down as she passed the little group, but she could not see exactly what was happening. Inside, she peered cautiously through the window. She was pretty sure they were taking money off the kid.

A minute later, Carol came into the shop.

'What's keeping you?' she moaned. 'All through lunch you couldn't wait, and now you're dawdling.'

'I *know*,' said Trisha. 'But I want to *buy* something.'

'Well buy it by yourself,' said Carol. 'I'm going. You can make your own way back to school.'

While they'd been arguing, the eight-year-old – fleeced –had been sent off with a threat of death if she ever breathed a word. As Carol stepped past the extortionists Heron was pushed backwards by a playful Lucy and slammed into her. Carol's bag fell to the ground. Jackie Heron, sneering up, saw who it was, *and* the look on her face.

'Sorry,' she said.

Carol looked at her bag.

'Well?' she said.

'It was an accident,' replied Jackie. 'She pushed me.'

'Pick it up,' said Carol. And when Heron hesitated: '*Pick it up!*'

Jackie put a brave face on it, but her sidekicks' leers cut deep. She was in a vicious mood when she spotted Judy Preston, trying to sneak past on the other side of the road. When Judy realized she'd been seen she did the only thing she could; she put her head down and ran.

'Right,' spat Jackie Heron. 'The sly little . . . Come on, girls! Let's teach her a lesson!'

Trisha, watching through the window, saw it all. She was a hundred yards behind them as they pounded after Judy. She knew now *exactly* what was going on.

When she got into school, Judy Preston did not worry about the rules. She raced down a corridor as fast as she could go. Halfway along it, with Brenda and Lucy only yards behind, she knew she'd fallen into another Heron trap. For Jackie was in front of her, closing the pincher. She'd used another door. Half a minute later, Judy was trapped again, in the fifth form cloakroom.

'So,' panted Jackie. 'Thought you'd give us the slip did you, Judy? Well I'll tell you what we do to –'

Trisha Yates burst in.

'Leave her alone!' she said, elbowing Brenda to one side. 'She's –'

Jackie pushed her up against the wall, grabbing her lapels.

'Who do you think *you* are?' she said. 'The Bionic Woman?'

Trisha was surprisingly strong. And fast. She pushed her arms up and outwards, breaking Jackie's grip.

'Let go of me,' she said. She placed herself by Judy, protectively. 'Why don't you pick on someone your own size?'

Jackie and her girls began to move in.

'Like *you* for instance?'

Trisha was defiant.

'You won't find me a pushover, Bigmouth!'

'Oh won't we?' smiled Jackie, banging her head against the brickwork. 'We'll soon see about *that*!'

But Jackie Heron had picked her time badly. It was almost registration time, and two girls came into the cloakroom to collect their things. They were fifth formers, and they were curious. Two first year kids and Heron's lot: the situation was clear. Heron and Co. backed off, and prepared to leave. Heron hissed at Trisha: 'We'll see *you* after school.'

The two fifth formers approached as the bullies disappeared. One of them, a dark-haired girl with a banded sweater on, looked closely at Trisha's face.

'Is your name Yates?' she asked.

Trisha smoothed herself down.

'Yeah.'

'Carol Yates's sister?'

'Yeah.'

'Is everything all right?'

Trisha and Judy glanced at each other. This was not on. You couldn't have everyone joining in, could you?

'Yeah, course it is,' she said. 'Fine. Why – shouldn't it be?'

Now the fifth formers exchanged a look. Snotty bloody first years, they thought. Didn't know they were born.

'Jackie Heron, that's all,' said the girl. 'Was she giving you a bad time?'

'No. Why should she?'

The fifth formers gave it up as a bad job.

'You want to watch out for her, that's all,' said one. 'She's a troublemaker. *If* you give her the chance. If you have any sense –'

Oh Gawd, thought Trisha Yates. Lecture time. She interrupted.

'We can look after ourselves,' she said. 'Can't we, Judy?'

Judy was not half so certain. But she wasn't going to contradict her friend, that was for sure. Her friend. She really really hoped. She nodded in agreement. The big girls shrugged.

'Come on, Judy,' said Trisha Yates. 'We'd better dash. Bye!'

By the end of school-time Trisha Yates had lost a lot of confidence, although she wasn't prepared to admit it to Judy. They hung around the classroom as long as possible, until Mr Mitchell shooed them out, then they lurked in a corridor overlooking the playground. Trisha told Judy they were all talk – a bit like Tucker Jenkins – and she bet they didn't mean it anyway. She showed Judy the earrings she'd put on after the bell – 'it *is* after school-time,' she said – and told her she'd had her ears pierced at the age of seven; Carol had taken her. They both agreed the school was spooky, so quiet and empty, and they jumped when Mr Mitchell came upon them.

He chatted for a few minutes, told them to leave – and noticed Trisha's jewellery. He frowned.

'I didn't see them, did I Trisha?' he asked.

'No sir,' she said.

'Good.'

He smiled, frowned, and left. Trisha poked her tongue out after him, but she slipped them off and into her pocket. Two minutes later, Garfield the Grumpy, the school caretaker, put the girls outside so that he could lock up. Crunch time.

They were halfway across the playground, and just beginning to feel safe, when they spotted Heron and her gang. Safe nothing – it was an ambush. But luckily for them, Carol was also in the hunt. She was doing some late studying with Mary, the girl in the striped jersey, who'd told her all about the cloakroom scene. They were expecting something, and they'd kept a good lookout going on the yard. When they saw Trisha and Judy racing across the tarmac, then Jackie and her mates in hot pursuit, they didn't need a three-day briefing. They flew.

Trisha and Judy were fast, but they didn't know the school like Jackie did. They ducked and weaved, got cut off – and took a wrong turning. With a clattering of heels the nasties arrived.

'Right,' said Jackie Heron. 'I think we have a little unsettled business. *Haven't* we?'

Lucy and Brenda were dead quick. As Carol and Mary turned up, they slipped away. Never mind loyalty – who wanted a hammering? Heron tried to follow, and got chucked against a wall by Carol. She glowered, but stayed put.

'Have you been threatening these two?' said Carol, levelly.

'No.'

'She has,' said Trisha. 'And she's stolen Judy's pen.'

'Give,' said Carol. Jackie gave.

'Did you take anything else, you . . .?'

'No.'

'Twenty pence,' said Judy, shyly. 'She took it from my purse.'

'Hand it over.'

Jackie Heron was still defiant.

'I've spent it.'

But she gave up when it looked as if she might get hurt. Carol took the money and shoved her sideways.

'Now push off,' she said. 'And *don't* get any funny ideas about taking it out on these two. Got it?'

Jackie was beaten. She satisfied herself with a look of hatred and left. Trisha, though, still had something to put up with. A little tirade from Carol about what a fool she'd been, and why hadn't she taken any notice of Mary in the cloakroom, and why hadn't she told her form master, and so on.

'Oh, don't shout at *her*,' said Judy, guiltily. 'It was all my fault really.'

'Anyway,' said Trisha. 'That would be squealing, wouldn't it.'

Carol and Mary shook their heads despairingly.

'So?' said Carol. 'Would you rather be beaten up?'

'The likes of Heron,' said Mary, 'are vermin. They have to be shown up. And stepped on.'

'Got it?' said Carol. '*No more heroics!*'

It all sounded very sensible to Judy, but Trisha did not look so sure. Trisha was *very* independent, thought Judy. She smiled at her, shyly. Trisha smiled back. Judy felt good.

Carol almost giggled. What a waste of time, talking sense to sister dear.

'All right,' she said. 'If anything else like this happens again, just tell *someone*, right? Even if it's only me or Mum. Or *your* Mum, love,' she said to Judy. 'Promise?'

Why not?

They nodded. Promise.

'Ah well,' said Carol, resignedly. 'Let's go home to tea.'

They did. And Judy enjoyed hers so much her mother felt better than she had for days. Perhaps the worst was over.

CHAPTER FOUR

Justin Time

Even if the kids of One Alpha agreed on nothing else, it was generally accepted that Justin Bennett was a wet. He looked like a girl, he hardly spoke to anyone, and he moped. What's more, his father dropped him off at school every morning, even if the sun was shining. In the big red 3.5 litre. Soppy *and* stuck up.

So when Tucker and Benny came zooming through the playground on their way to the swimming bath, they didn't hesitate when they saw him walking sedately along in front of them. With manic roars they screamed up behind him, knocked his schoolbag to the ground, and kicked it all round the yard. Books, pencils and swimming gear everywhere. Then on they zoomed, whooping crazily.

Tucker reached the pool door first and tugged smartly at the handle. It burst open with more force than he expected – because Grumpy Garfield was pushing from the other side. He had a mop in his hand and his normal ultra-friendly expression on his face. He was a grouch.

'Here! What d'you think you're playing at?' he snarled. 'Swinging on that door like that. You'll have the hinges off. Get back!'

'All right,' said Tucker. 'You don't have to push.'

Mr Garfield's old face got even more irascible.

'Don't you talk to me like that!' he said.

'Like what!' said Tucker. Some people!

'Giving me lip. I won't have it!'

'I wasn't *giving* it,' said Tucker. 'I only –'

'How long do you think this door would last?' continued Mr Garfield, pushing it to and fro, 'if people like you keep swinging on it?'

'We was only *opening* it,' said Benny Green.

'Oh no you weren't.' He fixed Benny with a beady stare. Probably vaguely remembering telling him off for his ball on the first day. 'I've had my eye on you,' he said. 'You were here last year, weren't you?'

'No!' said Benny.

'It must have been your brother, then.'

The other kids from One Alpha were straggling up. Benny grinned at them. We've got a right one here, it suggested. And *no* mistake.

'My brother doesn't go to this school,' he said.

The caretaker surveyed them all, with a look of distaste.

'You can't come in without a teacher,' he said. 'You can wait out here until one comes. Bunch of hooligans, the lot of you. You don't deserve the amenities we've got. You don't deserve them.'

He went inside, leaving Tucker jumping up and down scratching his armpits and doing his world famous gorilla act. Mr Mitchell walked through the crowd behind him and tapped him on the head with a rolled-up towel.

'All right, Jenkins,' he said. 'We all know where you're descended from. Lead in, boys, and get changed.'

Most of the boys were dead eager – even those who could not swim – so they were changed in a flash. Tucker and Benny looked a bit like pirates, Benny with his medallion on his chest and Jenkins in a pair of sawn-off jeans instead of trunks. Once they were ready, they began to get impatient.

'Where's Old Mitch?' said Tucker. 'The lesson'll be over before he's changed.'

'You can't win in this place,' said Benny. 'That Frosty Foster moans if you're late getting ready, and Mitchell keeps us hanging about.'

'He's probably getting his water wings on,' laughed Tucker.

'Can you swim?'

'Yeah, course I can. I can do anything, Ben. I'm Bionic. You any good?'

Benny said modestly: 'Well. I swum for my last school.'

'Gawd,' said Tucker, in mock disgust. 'Ain't there *any* sport you're not good at?'

'Yeah! Netball!'

Mr Mitchell arrived in time to prevent a brawl developing, with another master. They were both in swimming trunks and tracksuit tops.

'Can we go, sir?' Tucker was already making for the footbaths.

'Jenkins! Come back here!'

'Oh, sir, it's freezing hanging about here.'

He got the big warning from Mr Mitchell's eyes. He didn't fancy his class showing him up in front of another teacher, maybe.

'Shut up, Jenkins, unless you want to get dressed again. We do not go into the pool until *everyone* is ready.'

A chorus of moans went up, and shouts at Justin Bennett. Justin Bennett still had his shirt and tie on.

'Now,' said Mr Mitchell. 'This is Mr Malcolm, who takes swimming. I want you to listen very carefully to what he has to say.'

Mr Malcolm stepped forward.

'Before we go in,' he said. 'I just want to make one point absolutely clear.'

Jenkins leaned sideways to Benny and mocked the master's voice: 'Oh hwo wo hwo wo, la di dah!' he went.

'Did you say something, boy?'

Wounded innocence: 'Me sir! No sir!'

Mr Malcolm let it go.

'There is to be no fooling or larking about,' he went on. 'That means pushing, throwing, or 'helping' other people into the water.'

Mr Mitchell: 'Jenkins. Is that quite clear?'

'Ah hey, sir! Why pick on me?'

Old Mitch put on one of his looks.

'I don't *really* have to answer that, do I Jenkins?'

'Remember,' concluded Mr Malcolm. 'You will conduct yourselves in an orderly and disciplined manner. You will do *only* what I tell you to do, *and* you will do it immediately. Right. Is everybody ready?'

Even Justin was. Before they filed out, Mr Mitchell isolated Tucker.

'You can wait till everyone else has gone.'

A squawk of laughter from Benny.

'And so can you, Green. Now – everybody. Lead on.'

The class was combined for the swimming lesson with K1 – Alan Hargreaves's mob – so the three of them did manage to have a laugh. But it wasn't perfect, not like going to the baths on a Saturday, say. Mr Mitchell was regimenting the non-swimmers, who were messing about with arm-bands and learning to get their faces under, while Mr Malcolm made the others do two lengths each to see if they fitted his definition of people who could swim. They did manage to race each other for a few widths, but they couldn't scream and whoop and drown each other as they'd have liked to have done. Still – anything was better than lessons!

When they finally got the chance for a spot of horseplay it was because of Justin. He was walking along the pool edge like a little old lady, his shoulders all hunched up and looking shivery. He was a natural. With a quick glance round to see if they'd be spotted, Tucker, Benny and Alan half-crept, half-trotted up behind him. Before he knew what was happening, they were hustling him across the wet tiles. He managed to let out a feeble yelp or two, then he was flying towards the pale green water.

Retribution was at hand. Mr Garfield, the caretaker, had chosen that moment to walk past the end of the pool, mop and bucket at the ready. When he let out a hoarse yell, the Three Musketeers did not wait for a lecture. They dived into the pool and hoped to disappear.

No chance.

Mr Garfield came stomping down the side, his face set. Mr Malcolm and Mr Mitchell, realising that something was up, approached him. He was furious.

'It was them three there!' he shouted, pointing. 'Come on out! Young hooligans!'

'What's going on?' asked Mr Mitchell. He saw who was involved though, and signalled them out. They made reluctantly for the side of the pool.

'I'll tell you what's going on,' said Mr Garfield. He turned to Mr Malcolm, the 'master in charge'. 'You're not doing your job properly, that's what. Allowing them to fight and carry on. They should be banned out of this pool.'

Mr Malcolm was irritated. The caretaker had an unfortunate manner, even if he had a point this time.

'All right, Mr Garfield,' he said. 'There's no real harm done as far as I can –'

Mr Garfield waved his mop. Tucker and mates were out of the pool now, watching the developing aggro with interest.

'Only because I stopped them!' the caretaker said. 'I caught that one swinging on the door this morning! Hooligans!'

'I wasn't, sir!' said Jenkins. 'I was –'

'Jenkins!' said Mr Mitchell. 'Be quiet. And go and get dressed. All of you. I'll deal with you later.'

As he passed through the footbath, Tucker paused. The notes of anger in the staff voices were quite obvious.

'It's the likes of them that ruins it for the decent kids.'

'All *right,* Mr Garfield. We'll deal with it later.'

'Well I hope you do. My job's difficult enough without hooligans making it worse. Just you see that –'

'I said all *right.* We'll *deal* with it.'

Coo, thought Tucker. They'll be bashing each other next . . .

Alan went off to the changing room his class used, and Benny and Tucker – taking the opportunity to skip a shower – towelled themselves off and started to dress. They discussed the attitude of Mr Malcolm to the caretaker. Tucker reckoned they'd almost come to blows.

'Yeah,' said Benny. 'Well if it hadn't been for you they wouldn't have had to. And we wouldn't be in here now.'

'Beat it!' said Tucker. 'It wasn't my fault Old Misery came past.'

'It was your idea to throw Bennett in, though, wasn't it?'

'Huh,' said Tucker. 'He should've let us without kicking up a fuss!'

Obscurely convinced that it was all the victim's fault, he had a brainwave. He went to Justin's peg and took his trousers. Giggling, he started to pull them on.

50

'What you *doing?*' asked Benny. Tucker pulled his own on over Justin's. Benny got the point, and began to get the other clothes.

'No! Just his trousers! It'll be funnier!'

Benny put them back just as Tucker finished zipping up his own trousers. And just as Justin came in from the showers, wrapped up in a towel. Benny grabbed at it.

'What do Scotsmen wear under their kilts, Justin!'

Justin clung to it.

'How should I know! Leave me alone!'

The rest of the class were close on Justin's heels, and it was lecture time from Mr Mitchell. Benny and Tucker knew when to climb down, and they apologised profusely. It would never happen again, they said. Never, never, never. Tucker even made a salute, and said 'Scout's Honour'. Mr Mitchell did not smile.

'Somehow, Jenkins,' he said. 'I don't think they would *have* you in the Scouts. Have you apologised to Mr Bennett?'

Apologised to Justin? What lunacy was this!? But he did, and so did Green. It was almost nauseating, but the form tutor appeared to be satisfied.

'All right,' he said. 'We'll overlook it this time. But I'm warning you here and now. In future *anyone* found fooling about in the pool will be automatically banned. Is that clear?'

A mumbled Yes, sir.

'Is that *clear?*'

A shouted YES, SIR.

'Good. Then we'll say no more about it. Now hurry up and get dressed.'

Tucker and Benny already were.

'Can we go, sir?'

'Wait for the bell, Jenkins.'

As if by magic the bell went. Tucker gave Old Mitch a cheeky grin.

'Can we go *now*, sir!'

'Oh get *out*, Jenkins!'

Tucker and Benny raced for the classroom. They had something to attend to. Mr Mitchell noticed Justin, half-dressed, moping by his peg.

'Come on, Justin,' he said, encouragingly. 'Hurry up.'

'I can't sir,' muttered Justin. 'Somebody's stolen my trousers . . .'

It was bad enough losing his trousers, it was bad enough having to walk across the playground wrapped up in a large dressing gown beside a teacher. But Justin's humiliation was not over yet by a long chalk. As he stepped into the classroom, he was almost knocked over by the howls of derision. Shouts of Hello Sailor and Give us a flash, wolf-whistles and catcalls. Tucker bounced out of his seat and tried to lift the edge of the bathrobe.

'Doing your Scotsman act again, Justin!'

'All right, all right,' bellowed Mr Mitchell as he entered. 'Sit down everyone – and shut up.' When he'd achieved order he continued. 'Now. I suppose it's too much to expect that anyone knows what happened to Justin's trousers?'

Trisha Yates put her hand up, looking serious.

'Yes, Trisha?'

'He hasn't half got nice legs, sir!'

The girls howled.

'All right, Trisha, thank you. Jenkins? Green? Do you know anything about this?'

Tucker looked outraged.

'Me, sir!' He almost added 'How dare you', but thought better of it. Benny put his hand up.

'Is he certain he put them on this morning, sir?'

Everybody laughed, except Justin and Mr Mitchell. A slanging match developed between Benny and Justin, which the teacher cooled off quickly. He changed the subject to get off the jokes.

'Listen,' he said. 'Sit down, Justin, and we'll sort it out in a moment. I want to make a timetable announcement for tomorrow. As Mr Foster will not be here . . .' Loud cheers from the boys. '. . . there will be no gym.' Even louder cheers. 'Instead, an extra swimming period has been organised.'

The boys almost went crazy, but Trisha Yates stood up angrily.

'But sir, *we're* meant to have swimming tomorrow.'

'Yes, Trisha,' said Mr Mitchell. 'But you'll have gym instead.'

'But that's not fair, sir. Why should we suffer because of them?'

Tucker shouted: 'Because we're more important than you lot.'

Yeah, went the boys. *Rubbish,* went the girls.

'Huh,' spat Trisha. 'A big drip like you shouldn't need to go swimming. You're wet enough as it is!'

'Unfair or not,' shouted Mr Mitchell, 'it's a staffing problem and that is the way it will be. So nobody forget. Boys swimming, girls in the gym. I don't want anyone bringing the wrong frocks!'

A boy at the back stood up excitedly. He'd solved the riddle of the trousers.

'Sir! Look! Look out there!'

There was a mad stampede to the windows. On a broomstick, fluttering in the breeze, were Justin Bennett's grey bags. The class was in hysterics. Tucker and Benny looked through the window, then at each other.

Triffic!

Next day the scene in the swimming pool was more or less the same; noise, instruction, everybody having fun. Everybody, that is, but Justin Bennett. Benny had passed him in the playground earlier, after he'd got out of the 3.5 litre. He'd had a handkerchief stuffed up against his nose.

'All right, Justin?' Benny asked. 'You coming swimming today?'

'No!' said Justin. He didn't like Benny after yesterday, because he was certain he and Tucker were the culprits. 'I've got a cold,' he said.

'You know why that is, don't you?' laughed Benny, bouncing his plastic ball. 'Running around without your trousers on!'

Now Justin was sitting in the changing room, snuffling, while One Alpha and K1 shared another lesson. He was meant to be doing quiet study. But he was brooding on revenge.

His chance came through an accident – literally. One of the boys, running along the pool edge, cut his toe on something. Quite badly. Tommy Watson, a small boy in Alpha One who messed about with Tucker and Benny sometimes, ran to Mr Malcolm.

'Sir! Sir! Mr Mitchell said to tell you, sir! Winkle's cut his foot, sir!'

'*Who's* cut his foot?' said Mr Malcolm.

'Er. Graham, sir. He's bleeding, sir.'

Mr Malcolm looked across the pool to the injured boy. 'Right,' he told Watson. 'Go to the caretaker and get the first aid kit.' He glanced at all the swimmers, then crossed to his colleague. Winkle Graham's foot was dribbling bright blood everywhere.

'What happened?'

Mr Mitchell looked up.

'Cut his foot on the side of the pool somehow. Must be a loose tile.'

'*Another* one?' said Mr Malcolm. He raised his eyebrows. 'What *does* old Garfield do all the time? I'm *always* telling him . . .' He saw the curious faces of the boys and changed tack. 'Hmm,' he said. 'That'll need a stitch or two, I shouldn't be surprised.'

Tommy Watson turned up then with the first aid kit, although he hadn't found Mr Garfield. Benny was sent to get a bathrobe while the two teachers bandaged Winkle's foot. He stood up and tried to walk on it, but just went white and wobbly.

'Oh,' said Mr Mitchell. 'I think we're going to have to carry you, young man.'

Mr Malcolm turned to the pool and waved his arms around.

'I'm sorry, everyone! We'll have to clear the pool while we take young Graham to the medical centre. Everybody out! We'll resume when we return.'

There were groans aplenty, but the pool was cleared quite quickly, and everyone was waved into the changing rooms. Benny handed over the robe, Graham was wrapped up, and the masters placed his arms around their necks and helped him away. Benny raced through the footbath to join his mates.

When he reached the changing room he caught up with Tucker, who was standing near Justin. Justin was ignoring him, pretending to read his book.

'Hey, Ben,' said Tucker. 'Did you see old Winkle's foot? Flipping heck, it was a good job there were no sharks in there. They'd have gobbled him, no messing.'

He did an impersonation of a shark tearing someone's leg from off his writhing body. Most of the water in his hair was shaken over Justin and his book.

'Careful!' snuffled Justin. 'It's going on my book and uniform!'

'Oh, sorry,' said Tucker, shaking his head more vigorously. 'I didn't smell you sitting there!'

'You did it on purpose,' said Justin.

'I was only showing him how a shark eats its dinner!' He shook his head some more, towards Benny this time. But Benny snapped at him.

'Pack it in, Tucker.'

Tucker was surprised.

'What's up with you?'

Benny indicated his chest. It was bare.

'I've lost my medal. The one my uncle gave me.'

Tommy Watson and Tucker moved in close. Alan, who should have been next door, joined the party. 'Did you lose it in the pool?' he asked.

Benny reckoned he must have done, and Tucker said that that was that, then – it would've been sucked into the filters and mangled. The others rubbished him, but everyone agreed they'd have to be quick to save it. They hurried through the footbaths once more, and Alan stationed himself at the doorway as lookout. The others went to the pool to search.

The little waves on the pale green water distorted everything, but it wasn't many seconds before Tommy Watson spotted it. He should have been the lookout, perhaps – eyes like a coalhouse rat! Benny verified the find and dived cleanly in. Half a minute later he was climbing up the ladder in triumph, the medallion on its broken chain clutched in his hand. He passed it up to Tommy, who put it on a bench. And Tucker – the last of the English gentlemen – kicked Benny straight back into the pool and pelted him with polystyrene swimming floats!

Ace, thought Tommy Watson. He picked up the next bench along and hauled it to the side. Then he shoved Tucker in, whanged a float at his head, and shouted to Benny – who'd scrambled up the ladder – to help him. Between them they chucked the wooden bench at Tucker, missing his head by inches.

'Catch!'

Tommy Watson dived neatly over the floating bench and climbed on board. Terrific boat! Benny dashed to the wall for another one.

'Is it all clear, Alan?'

'Yeah,' said Alan, nervously. 'But I don't think you ought to.'

Rhubarb! Make hay while the sun shines! Benny shouted, Tucker shouted, Tommy Watson shouted.

And it was too much for Alan. He pounded down the poolside to Benny. The second bench went hurtling through the air, and Alan followed it in with a gigantic splash.

'Get in line,' cried Benny. 'We'll have a boat race!' And he was in there, too.

It wasn't many seconds before the rest of the boys were pouring from the changing rooms. They yelled and shouted as Oxford and Cambridge splashed and lumbered slowly along in the water. The air was white with polystyrene blocks. Justin Bennett, picking his way carefully past the footbath, poked his head round a corner of white-tiled wall.

And smiled.

It was a bear garden. It was endangering life and limb. It was forbidden. He went to find the caretaker.

The lookout was good – some of the more nervous boys had one eye out of the window despite the excitement in the pool – but it was not good enough. When the cry of 'caretaker' went up, the benches were jerked out of the pool, and the polystyrene floats were nearly all collected up. Benny and Alan and Watson and Tucker reckoned they'd have got away with it except for the state of the benches. They were soaking. Nothing to do except to sit on them. Try and make it look logical. Oh well. Good try.

Mr Garfield was puffing like a grampus. A grampus in a lousy temper.

'All right, you lot, that's it. I've warned you. I –' He looked at the benches. He could hardly believe such badness. 'You've had them in the water!' he said. 'You've had these benches in the water!'

'Us!' said Tucker. 'Nah, we haven't, have we lads!'

'They're soaking wet!'

It could have been a long and pointless argument, but Mr Malcolm turned up then, and the caretaker could carry it on with someone he *really* didn't like. The boys were chased off into the changing rooms, and only picked up scraps of it. But a real dingdong started, with Mr Garfield accusing Mr Malcolm of not keeping the pupils in control, (Or hooligans, as he preferred to call them.)

'If you lot did your job properly,' he said bitterly, 'this sort of thing wouldn't happen.'

'And if you did *your* job properly,' said Mr Malcolm furiously, 'and made sure there were no loose tiles round the pool, that young boy would not need three stitches in his foot. *Nor,*' he added, 'would I have had to leave the building in the first place!'

Mr Garfield stormed off to take it out on the flower beds. Mr Malcolm stormed into the boys.

'Jenkins! Green! Here! NOW!'

They stood in front of him. Even Tucker wasn't feeling smart.

'Who else was with you?' No response. Mr Malcolm began to swell.

Tommy Watson, fearing to see a master explode over a wide area, did his Boys Own Paper bit. Out of fear, more than anything. He stepped forward.

'Me, sir,' he said quietly.

'And?'

'Alan Hargreaves from K1.'

Mr Malcolm wound down a fraction.

57

'I'll deal with him later,' he said. He wound down some more. He didn't relish frightening little boys, not even fools like these. He spoke to Tucker Jenkins.

'Well, Jenkins. What were you told yesterday?'

Tucker's head was on his chest.

'Be banned if we messed around, sir.'

'And do you think that a fair punishment under the circumstances?'

'I suppose so, sir.'

'You others. Do you agree?'

They nodded. Mr Malcolm relaxed.

'Right,' he said. 'You will be banned for three weeks. And I'm only being so lenient because I did not see exactly what happened myself. I –'

'*Lenient!*' exploded Tucker. And regretted it.

'Yes, Jenkins, lenient. But as you do not think so, you can do three hours detention as well on top of it. *All* of you.'

When he had gone, Tucker turned bitterly on Tommy Watson. For dropping Alan Hargreaves in it. Watson was in no mood for that. He had a go at Tucker for getting them detention to add on to the ban. Justin Bennett, from his bench, said smugly: '*I* think you got off too lightly. *I* think you should have been banned for good.'

'Look, pack it in, Bennett,' said Tucker. 'If it hadn't been for you making all that aggro we'd have been all right.'

Justin was pretty pleased with the way his revenge had gone. He said confidently: 'Well, you shouldn't pick on me, should you!'

'I'll do more than pick on you in a minute,' said Tucker. But his heart wasn't in it. He was choked. He went to his place.

'See you later, Tucker!' said Benny. He was already dressed.

'Hey! Wait a minute. Where are you going in such a – Benny!'

Tucker reached morosely for his clothes. He lifted his shirt, then it dawned on him.

'Hey!' he said, in shock. Then horror. 'Hey! Someone's nicked me trousers!'

A yell of laughter went up from the boys. Justin Bennett, very daring, brought a robe across.

'I think you might be needing this,' he said. And laughed. Tucker aimed a kick at him. He threw himself onto the bench and folded his arms. He felt a hundred percenter. Pillock.

There was quite a crowd in the playground when he walked through. The usual cries of derision, the chants of Hello Sailor. Some of the girls came out, and Trisha tried to pull the robe aside and expose his frailty. There was a shout from on high.

Benny's head was poking out of the classroom window, split from ear to ear with a grin. In his hand was a broomstick.

And on it, was a pair of trousers. Fluttering merrily.

Justin Bennett nearly bust a button.

CHAPTER FIVE

The Hamster

One of the things that got on Trisha Yates's wick about being a schoolkid was the way it made everybody pick on you. Just because you were in a uniform with long white socks, just because you were herded up like an animal and jammed in a classroom every day, just because you had to spend your waking hours with pigs like Tucker Jenkins and his mates, people treated you like dirt. Some of the kids reckoned Old Mitch was nice, but she didn't. Some of the kids reckoned Mrs Munroe was all right, but not Trisha. All teachers were the same to her – horrible.

With one exception. There was a biology master, a man called Mr Rankin, whom all the other kids laughed their socks off over. The general opinion was that he was so old he should have been boxed years ago; he was like Dracula's grandad. He had grey hair, and bushy eyebrows, and a pair of goggles that wouldn't stay on his nose. He stooped about in scruffy gear and a long white coat and he spoke all sort of posh and old-fashioned, like something out of Dickens or a play by Shakespeare. He was a fossil, a relic, a wreck. Trisha liked him.

And over a couple of weeks, subtle and crafty as a lynx so that no one would notice her, she wormed her way in with him. She cleared up around his lab, she tidied his desk (which always needed it). She finally asked him if she could help him in the dinner hour sometimes. Mr Rankin, surprised at first, became enthusiastic. Yes, Trisha, certainly my dear! My my this is an honour! This is a privilege! Now what a noble-hearted, generous gesture to be sure! Well well! He almost frightened Trisha off – he did go on a bit. But she had to admit it – she thought he was really sweet. And there were the animals to think about, the guinea pigs and the white rat, the lizards and the praying mantis. The hamster. Trisha fancied playing with the animals, watching them and getting to have a stroke. It would be worth it for that alone.

One of the people who liked to pick on her most, and push her around, and make her life a misery, was her sister Carol. She didn't do it in a nasty way, she didn't hate her or anything like that. But she was persistent. She never missed an opportunity. On the first day Trisha was allowed to help Mr Rankin, she jumped in with both feet. It started because her little sister was bolting her food, anxious to get back to the lab and help. Carol pulled a disgusted face.

'Mum!' she said, with a pained note in her voice. '*Do* something!'

Mrs Yates said comfortably: 'Trisha, you'll make yourself sick eating like that.'

'She's certainly making me feel sick,' said Carol. 'We should get her a trough and make the little pig feel at home.'

Trisha was too busy filling her mouth with chips and sausage to reply. Her mother looked at her bulging cheeks.

'What's the rush to get back to school, darling?' she asked. 'It's not like you.'

Trisha swallowed, almost tearing the lining of her throat out as she did so.

'I'm helping Mr Rankin.'

'Mr Rankin? And who might Mr Rankin be?'

Carol put on a shocked look.

'He's some old dodderer who teaches biology,' she said. 'He's *senile!*'

'He is not!' said her sister, furiously. She felt like sticking her fork in Carol. She was *always* getting at her.

Carol poked the tip of her tongue out. A ladylike insult.

'Of course he is,' she said. 'He walks around in bicycle clips all day.'

'So! That doesn't make him senile!'

'It does if he hasn't got a bike!'

Mrs Yates could never understand how heated Trisha could get over nothing. She was on her feet now, her face blazing.

61

'He *has* got a bike and you've no right to –'

'Trisha!' said Mrs Yates sharply. 'Sit down immediately. Can't you see your sister's teasing you?'

Trisha sat down heavily.

'Well she's stupid,' she said. 'She's always making fun of me. It's not fair.'

'Yes dear, I'm sure. Now I'll ask you again. Who is Mr Rankin and why are you helping him?'

Trisha gave Carol a look that *dared* her to interrupt.

'He's our biology tutor, Mum. Oh Mum, he's *ever* so nice. He's not like the other teachers, he doesn't push you around, you know. And he makes you feel. Sort of . . . you know . . .' She felt silly, and gave a shrug. 'Oh, I don't know. He's just sort of . . . different.'

'Yeah,' said Carol slyly. 'He wears bicycle clips. The way she's carrying on, Mum, you'd think she had a crush on him!'

Trisha stood up, leaving her plate half full. Despite her mother's protests she got ready to go. But as she passed the sink, Mrs Yates noticed something. Trisha was wearing earrings.

She was all for making her remove them on the spot, but Trisha got even more upset.

'It's the lunch time, Mum,' she said. 'You're *allowed* to wear them in the lunch time. Aren't you, Carol?'

Surprisingly, Carol backed her up – although they both knew it wasn't strictly true. 'She'll be all right, Mum,' she said. 'As long as she remembers to take them out. It *is* the dinner hour.'

Mrs Yates relented. She took a five pound note from the sideboard pot and Trisha pocketed it. It was an instalment towards the school holiday. Trisha said Goodbye to her mother, glared at her sister – and left.

She had a great time in the lab, scouring out the inside of some test tubes and glass jars with a long wire brush while Mr Rankin pottered around behind her. He was a funny old fellow, she had to admit – a cross between a mad professor in a comic and a nice old grandad. He hummed and made various odd noises while he worked. When

Trisha had polished the last tube she turned to him and told him she'd finished. Mr Rankin came shambling over in his lab coat.

'My word, Trisha,' he beamed. 'Well done, well done indeed.' He pushed his wobbly specs back up his nose. 'I never expected anybody could get them *that* clean. Absolutely splendid.'

Trisha felt great. If Mum went on like that when she'd done the washing up she might volunteer more often!

'Ooh, thank you, Mr Rankin.'

'The thanks are entirely due on my part,' he said. 'Splendid effort. Now . . . er . . . what was I going to . . .? Ah yes, lunch. I think I ought to be hungry. Yes. Yes, I am. Ah, my dear, if only we could be like the snakes, eh?

Trisha tried to appear polite, but she was baffled. He bumbled on.

'Such sensible creatures, snakes, aren't they? They don't eat very often, but when they do . . . ah.'

Maybe he knew something about snakes that she didn't. Horrible things, Trisha thought.

'Is there anything else I can do, please?'

'Hmm. Are you sure you have the time?'

'Oh, yeah, plenty of time.'

'Well! How good of you!' He went to a bench and indicated a small empty cage. It was filthy. Caked. He twanged the wire bars with his fingernail. 'I had been *hoping*,' he said. 'That someone might volunteer to clean . . . *that*. Disgusting, isn't it? Left far too long. It hasn't been used for some considerable time.'

Well, if you're going to volunteer, thought Trisha. Might as well do the nasty bits as well.

'That's all right,' she said. 'Leave it to me.'

He shook his head, apparently in admiration.

'Very well,' he said. 'If you say so. I'll go and get some lunch then. Marvellous. Oh . . . Trisha . . . did I tell you what you should and should not touch?'

'Yes, Mr Rankin. Not to touch the –'

'Splendid. Good. Excellent. Yes, I won't be very long, dear.'

How nice to be trusted. Trisha grinned. She really liked him.

The cage was a smelly article, and Trisha had only just begun properly to shift the dirt when she heard the door behind her open. It was Judy Preston.

The two girls got on well now, they were sort of friends. Trisha thought that Judy was rather serious; she didn't read love magazines or try on make-up and stuff – and she was also rather posh. But she wasn't at all stuck up, and she could be a laugh. They were quite good mates. But this was *too* much. It was neither the time nor the place. No one but the lunchtime lab assistant was allowed in, for starters. She didn't say anything, but she was hardly welcoming.

'Er. Hello, Trisha.'

'What do you want?'

'I . . . er. Came to see you.'

'You're not supposed to be here. Mr Rankin only allows me in here. To help him.'

'Oh,' said Judy. She looked down-in-the-mouth. 'Please let me stay for a little.'

'Why?'

Trisha pretended to be concentrating on the cage at the half-full sink. Judy moved to a row of animal cages on a bench. She stared in at the hamster.

'Because we're . . . you know.' She had an inspiration. 'And . . . and I thought I might do an article for the school magazine. On the animals. Can I take one out?'

Trisha was irritated. She wasn't allowed to touch the animals, naturally. But she didn't want to admit that, now did she? She did some vigorous scrubbing.

'No. No one can take them out.'

'Not even you?'

Judy's tone was sweet and innocent – everything *about* her was *always* sweet and innocent – but there was a deliberate challenge, all the same. Trisha Yates was a sucker for challenges, Judy knew.

'Well, if I wanted to I could,' she replied. 'But I don't. I'm too busy.'

Judy came out into the open.

'Huh. I bet you're not allowed to take them out.'

'I *am*. I'm Mr Rankin's assistant. I can do *anything*.'

'Prove it. There you are, you *can't*.'

Trisha dried her hands on a towel and marched to the row of cages. She gave Judy a look.

'Just a little hold,' she said. 'I told you, I'm *busy*. Some people!'

She nervously opened the front of the cage and put her hand in. She guessed there was a proper way to pick up small animals, but she did not know what it was. The hamster was very soft and wriggly; she was afraid of hurting it. But when she handed it to Judy she told her airily: 'You hold it like *this*.'

'Oh,' breathed Judy, delighted. 'Isn't he *gorgeous*.'

Trisha knew something awful would happen and it did. The door opened and Miss Clarke came in. She was a biology teacher like Mr Rankin – only she wasn't like him at all. She was neat, and smart, and efficient, and strict. Thank heavens she was carrying a clipboard, and she was preoccupied. Before she noticed the girls across the lab, Judy had bundled the hamster back into the cage and they'd turned their backs on it, to face the teacher. She saw them.

'What are you two doing here?' she asked. Her face, framed in straight golden hair, was severe. So was her voice. Trisha swallowed.

'Helping Mr Rankin, Miss Clarke.' Judy, rather petrified, kept her eyes down and her mouth shut.

'Helping him?'

'His lunchtime assistant, Miss.'

Miss Clarke's beady eyes searched Trisha's face. Her expression grew even frostier.

'Are you wearing earrings?' she asked.

Ouch! thought Trisha. She nodded. And got a short harangue on rules and regulations.

'I . . . I thought it would be all right,' she said. 'In the lunch hour I mean, Miss.'

'Well you thought wrong, didn't you? Take them off.' Trisha did so. 'And apply to me for detention at four o'clock tomorrow. What's your name?'

G.D.G.H.—C

'Trisha Yates, Miss. Form One Alpha.'

'And you?'

'I'm her friend, Miss. Judy Preston, Miss. Form One Alpha.'

Miss Clarke looked suspicious.

'Does Mr Rankin know you're *both* here?'

Judy looked anxiously at Trisha. Trisha swallow again.

'Yes Miss,' she said. 'He's just gone for some lunch, Miss.'

'Hm,' went Miss Clarke. 'It's a wonder he remembered. Well, carry on with what you were doing. And don't touch anything you shouldn't.'

'Thanks Trisha,' said Judy, when she'd gone.

'I had to say that, didn't I? Or I'd have got even *more* detention for letting you in here.'

The tone was hardly friendly. Judy knew quite well she'd overstayed her welcome. Not that she'd ever had one!

'I'd better go,' she said.

'Yeah,' said Trisha, moodily. She stomped towards the sink. Great, she thought. The ruin of a ruddy good dinner hour. That Judy Pres –

'Trisha!' It was almost a scream. Judy Preston was looking at the hamster cage in horror. The wire door was hanging open. And the hamster was gone.

In the first few seconds, as they frantically searched the floor with their eyes, they had a stroke of luck. They saw the little brownish beast scuttling under a tall bookshelf. It was their first stroke of luck. And their last.

'Quick,' said Trisha. 'The other end. I'll pull the shelves out, and you grab it, right? And for God's sake don't squash it!'

It was a pretty dim thing to try and do, because the bookshelf was about six feet tall, and packed with books. But they were too panicky to think straight. Trisha began to ease it forward, with scant regard for the laws of gravity, or balance.

'Look out! Look out!'

Too late. Slowly at first, then at ridiculous speed, the shelves toppled. A thunderous cascade of books drummed onto the floor and the bookshelf banged to a halt against the corner of a bench. Trisha saw the round hindquarters of the hamster disappearing through a ventilator grill.

'Judy!' she squeaked. 'The prep room! Quick! It's going through the wall!'

They blundered through the doorway into the prep room, and scanned the floor for the tiny animal. Nothing. Trisha turned on Judy, her anger spilling over.

'It's all your fault this happened!' she said. 'It's all your fault, Judy Preston!'

'It's not! It's not! You shouldn't have left the cage door open!'

'Well who wanted to take the hamster out in the first place? I'm not supposed to touch the animals! It's ruined everything!'

'Trisha!' said Judy. Trisha followed her pointing finger. The outside door to the prep room was open. It led on to a small area of grass and shrubs. Trisha dashed through. She ran about like a headless chicken. Judy stood in the doorway, worrying.

'There's no point,' she said. 'You'll never find it out here. And we don't even know if it came out, do we? It's hopeless.'

They kicked around the bushes, feeling miserable. In the end Trisha admitted defeat and they went back inside. She was depressed.

'Look,' she said. 'I'm ever so sorry I shouted at you just now. I didn't really mean it.'

'That's all right.'

'But what are we going to *do?*'

'I don't *know.*'

They stood beside the bookshelf, biting their lips. Judy began to pull it upright. 'I suppose we'll just have to tell him,' she said. 'It *was* an accident.'

'No!' said Trisha. 'I can't. He'll never let me help him again!'

Judy shrugged.

'He'll know soon enough anyway,' she said. 'When he gets back and sees the cage.' She stopped. Her mouth dropped open. 'Unless,' she breathed. 'Unless . . . Oh, Trisha – why don't we replace the hamster!'

Trisha's eyes widened in hope.

'How!?'

'The pet shop in London Road. We could –'

'How much are they?'

'I don't *know*. But they can't be *very* much. Oh . . . oh, I've got no money. Have you?'

Trisha's heart sank.

'No, I – Yes!' She thrust her hand into her blazer pocket. 'Mum gave me some for the school holiday! Here!'

She gave Judy a five pound note. She could have hugged her.

'Hurry!' she said. 'I'll clear this mess up. *Hurry!*'

Although Trisha expected to be caught out at any moment, nothing happened. She got the shelves upright, pushed them back against the wall, and started to pick up the books and slot them in. She had no idea what order they ought to be in, but she did not care. That was the least of her worries just at present, and anyway, it might be ages before anybody noticed. By the time she'd got it to rights again she had her breath back and her heartbeat under control. She checked that everything looked normal. It did. She returned to the sink. There wasn't much time to finish the cage.

For Judy Preston, things did not go so well. When she thundered up to the pet shop and tried the door it did not budge. Then she saw the notice: Closed for lunch: 12.15 to 1.15. She looked at her wristwatch. Ten minutes to wait. She almost blew up. She hopped about in panic and impatience. Oh hurry *up*, she thought, hurry up! Ages later she looked at her watch again. Less than a minute had passed! Judy, desperate, went for a very brisk walk around the block.

Trisha was beginning to panic badly after fifteen minutes, too. She jumped with relief when the door handle went.

'Judy!'

But no. It was Miss Clarke, back with her clipboard.

'Oh,' she said. 'Are you still here?'

'Yes, Miss.'

Miss Clarke walked so close to the empty hamster cage that Trisha nearly collapsed. She splashed noisily in the sink in the hope of distracting her attention. But the teacher was absorbed. She checked a few things, went to the cupboard, and left.

Oh Gawd, Trisha said frantically to herself. Come *on*, Judy. Come *on*.

When the shop assistant switched the sign to Open, Judy Preston burst through the door like a blonde bullet.

'Yes, young lady,' said the startled assistant. 'What can –'

'Hamsters! Do you have any hamsters, please?'

'Well, yes. They're over there. No. There. That's it.'

Judy looked intently through the glass into the tank. There was one that looked perfect. Right size, right colour.

'Any partic –'

'That one! Yes. Please. Oh *please* hurry!'

The assistant gave her a funny look and produced an oblong cardboard box. She took the mesh off the cage and put her hand in. As she did so another assistant turned up from the back of the shop.

'Telephone, love.'

The first lady smiled at Judy, and gave the girl the box.

'That hamster in the corner,' she said. 'Give it to this young lady, will you?'

As the shop-girl reached into the tank, Judy fumbled in her blazer pocket for the five pound note. A mistake, because the hamsters had moved around. The one in the corner now was bright yellow, not cream-brown. The girl picked it up and popped it into the cardboard carrying box.

'There,' she said. Judy took the box, handed over the money, and set off towards the door.

'Hey!' said the shopgirl. 'Your change!'

Judy returned and took it. Then she fled.

Running with a live animal in a cardboard box is not easy if you don't want to hurt it. Judy kept feeling it sliding about and had to slow down. Then she'd find herself going fast again, and got pangs of guilt. Poor little thing! And anyway – what if it got injured? Or died! She slowed down, sped up, slowed down. It was *awful*

As she crossed the last part of the school grounds to the science block a new, and totally unexpected, hazard loomed up. Jackie Heron and friends spotted her, and began to run.

Hamster or no hamster, Judy put on a terrific burst of speed. But Heron and Co. had got a start, and were on a good angle to cut her off. They probably thought it was a fine chance to settle old scores, what's more. As she reached the science block doorway, they surrounded her.

'Well, well,' panted Jackie Heron. 'What's the hurry, little girl? What have we got here?'

'Nothing!' said Judy. 'Leave me alone!'

'Nothing, eh?' Heron snatched the box and put it to her ear. 'We'll see, shall we?'

Down the pathway, round a corner, came Mr Rankin. He did not see anything. His head was in a book. Judy half shouted to him.

'Excuse me, sir!'

Jackie Heron's head snapped round. Judy lifted the box smartly from her hands, pushed open the door, and darted through. Half a minute later she burst into the laboratory.

'Oh, Judy!' said Trisha, dead with relief. 'Where've you *been!* Did you get it?'

Judy held out the box.

'Only just, though. Mr Rankin's right behind me!'

They nipped to the cage and Trisha fumbled with the box lid and the gate. As the hamster popped out onto the sawdust she gasped.

'Stupid! It's the wrong colour!'

Judy could only stare. The door opened and Mr Rankin bumbled in, his nose still in his book.

'Sorry I'm late, Trisha,' he said. 'I had one or two things to do after lunch, and then I had to go and . . .' He had put the book down and walked towards them. He was looking into the cage. 'My word, you have done well. I – Hello! That's odd!'

As he stooped forward for a better view, there was a squeaking. *Behind* Trisha and Judy. Mr Rankin's eyes left the cage and followed the sound.

'What on earth?' he said.

There, was the original hamster. The stray. The runaway. Crawling around the floor as happy as a sandboy. Not three feet away.

'*Now* who's stupid?' muttered Judy Preston. 'It must have been here all the time.'

Mr Rankin had picked the animal up gently by the loose skin behind its head. Without a word he put it into the cage and withdrew the other one. The yellow one. He held it up and looked at it.

'I . . .' said Trisha. 'I suppose we'd better tell you what happened, sir.'

'Yes,' said Mr Rankin. 'I think you'd better.'

'Well,' said Trisha. She glanced at Judy. 'Er . . . we took the hamster out of its cage.'

'Just to have a *look,*' said Judy.

'It got away and we couldn't catch it.'

Mr Rankin raised his grey and bushy brows. Judy gabbled: 'Trisha didn't want you to find out, so we thought we'd get you another hamster. But . . . but everything got in a muddle and I got the wrong colour.'

She blushed. It sounded very silly.

Trisha said humbly: 'We're terribly sorry, sir. We shouldn't have taken it out of the cage.'

The biology master left them silent for a moment. Then he held the yellow hamster aloft. 'Oh dear,' he said. 'Your plan certainly did go wrong. Not only did you get the wrong colour – you got the wrong sex. Mister . . . would have become Missis!'

He put the hamster into the cage and clicked the door firmly. He put on a schoolmasterly expression.

'Now,' he asked them. 'Would either of you think it unreasonable of me if I were to report you both to Mrs Munroe?'

They shook their heads. They'd asked for it. But Mr Rankin let his face relax.

'No, neither would I,' he said. 'And the only thing that prevents me is the fact that you tried to put things right. A lot of children would just have sloped off and pretended it hadn't happened. You did not.'

'We couldn't have done *that*, sir!' said Trisha.

'Obviously not,' he smiled. 'So – as there's no real harm done, I think the best thing we can do is forget the whole thing. Just this once though – another time and I won't be quite so lenient.'

They could hardly believe their luck, and they thanked him fervently. But there was even better to come. Mr Rankin found out where Judy had bought the hamster, gave her £1.25 to cover what she'd paid for it – and said he would take it back to the shop in London Road. Trisha was able to have her whole five pounds back – the end of another worry. As they left the lab, he even asked her if she was coming back next day. Trisha hesitated.

'Er. I'd rather not if you don't mind, sir,' she said.

Mr Rankin almost laughed.

'Oh yes, I was forgetting. You're going to want some spare time, aren't you? Miss Clarke told me about the . . .' He touched his ear-lobe. 'Not your day is it, Trisha?'

Rueful look.

'No, sir.'

'No. Goodbye, both of you.'

Walking down the corridor, Judy said to Trisha: 'I can see why you like him, Trisha. He's so understanding. I couldn't see Miss Clarke letting us off like that.'

'You ought to include her in your article about animals,' Trisha replied.

'Why?'

'Because she's a cow.'

'Trisha!'

'Well, I ask you! It was the lunch hour. I don't think this school should have any right to tell you what to do in your own time.'

Judy thought.

'Now *that's* something I could write about in the school magazine,' she said. 'Do you think they'd let me?'

Trisha was scornful.

'Nah. They'd more than likely censor it. Better stick to animals. Safer.'

Safer! Judy's face split into a grin.

'Are you *sure*!' she said.

CHAPTER SIX

Do or Die

Ever since the incident in the swimming pool, Justin Bennett had wanted to do something to redeem himself in the eyes of Tucker Jenkins and Benny Green. It wasn't that they treated him any differently – they more or less ignored him, like they had always done – but he felt he ought to make a gesture. Although in one way he'd made his point, and taught them a lesson, in another way he felt bad. He felt a creep and a weed. And Justin didn't want to feel like that. He'd much rather be friends.

Secretly, he envied Tucker and Benny, because they didn't give a damn. Tucker found it impossible to walk across a street or a room without messing about, or tripping up, or knocking someone over, and Benny was ready for anything. He didn't mind being mocked, either, a thing which Justin hated. Earlier this morning, for instance, he'd turned up in a brand new blazer – several sizes too big because his Mum wanted room for him to grow into it – and the class had ragged him rotten. Benny had given as good as he'd got – but it hadn't apparently upset him. Justin admired that like mad.

The problem was – how to get to know them without sucking up, or sounding like a drip, or looking like a fool? He couldn't just join in with them, because they wouldn't let him. In any case, a lot of the things they did were so daft and dangerous they made him go quite weak. Like the stunt they were pulling now, with Benny's chisel. Blood would flow. It had to. And it was all being done under the nose of the teacher.

Mr Parkes, the woodwork master, was Welsh, and canny. He did his job properly, and he prided himself on losing as few finger ends and eyeballs as humanly possible. He'd told them all about woodwork tools, and how dangerous they could be. Especially chisels. Ah well, thought Justin, glancing sideways to where Benny and

Tucker were standing. Even Mr Parkes could not be everywhere at once . . .

Thunk. Benny's chisel, chucked by Tucker Jenkins, stuck firmly into the plank they'd propped against the wall. Tucker raised his arms in triumph.

'And there it is!' he crowed. 'Another great throw for the champion!'

Justin winced. It amazed him how much noise Jenkins could make and get away with it. Mr Parkes was absorbed at the other side of the woodwork room, helping a more conscientious boy.

'Three-two to you,' said Benny. 'Here. My go.'

The chisel hit the side of the upright plank and bounced sideways into a waste bin. There was a metallic clatter.

'What's going on over there?' called Mr Parkes. Tucker went on chiselling. Benny walked to the bin, looking concerned and innocent.

'I dropped my chisel, sir.'

Mr Parkes picked it up and touched the point with his thumb.

'For goodness sake, Green. Be more careful. These things are *sharp*, you know.'

He walked to Benny's bench and picked up the piece of wood in which he was cutting rebates.

'Hmm, not bad. But your saw cut is deeper than the rebate you want. You'd have to fill it. Try again.'

Tucker was sharing the bench. Mr Parkes picked up his piece of work and sighed.

'Short of firewood in your house, Jenkins?'

'How do you mean, sir?' (As if he didn't know).

'That's all this is fit for,' said Mr Parkes. 'You've chiselled much too deep. What's the point of making guidelines if you don't follow them?' He tapped Tucker lightly on the head with the wood. 'Try again, Jenkins. Try again.'

Tucker did his monkey act at the master's retreating back – and an appalling imitation of a Welsh accent.

'Try again, Jenkins. Try again! That's all he ever says. I must have chiselled out that rebate a hundred times.'

'Twice, it was.'

'Who cares?' said Jenkins. 'I hate woodwork.'

A small smile from Benny, chiselling away.

'You hate everything.'

'No I don't. I like swimming.' Jenkins noticed that Justin, on the next bench along, was watching them. He scowled. 'Except that certain people get us barred out,' he said.

Benny glanced at Justin's pale and anxious face. He felt sorry for him sometimes.

'It was us that lobbed the benches in, Tucker.'

Tucker had fixed Justin with a malevolent stare.

'Yeah,' he said. 'But who gave the whisper to that old caretaker? Eh, Justin?'

Justin looked down to his work hurriedly as Tucker lounged towards him. Jenkins pushed him sideways by the shoulder and Justin's chisel slipped out of the rebate he was cutting.

'Oh,' said Tucker. 'Look what you've done. You'll just have to try again, Bennett! Try again!'

The woodwork teacher was still occupied, so Tucker took up a throwing stance and chucked his chisel at the plank target.

'Flipping heck,' he said to Benny, over his shoulder. 'Did you see that one? Dead centre!'

Benny joined him.

'Anyone could do that.'

'Go on, then.'

But Mr Parkes was coming closer. Benny turned to his bench.

'Nah,' he said. 'I don't feel like it.'

Tucker went back to his own work.

'Laid any good eggs yet?' he said, after a moment.

'What?'

'That's what chickens do, isn't it?' He did a broody hen noise. Benny was riled.

'I'd do anything *you'd* do,' he said.

Tucker smirked. He enjoyed provoking people.

'You wouldn't,' he said. 'You're not as tough as me.'

Justin had stopped work altogether. It wasn't often you saw Tucker and Benny almost quarrelling. Now Tucker was deep in thought.

'I bet you wouldn't swim in a shark-infested river,' he said.

Justin was disappointed. That was just silly. Even Benny laughed.

'Neither would you!' he said.

Justin butted in: 'Sharks don't live in rivers.'

'They do sometimes,' retorted Tucker. 'They swim up from the sea. I seen a programme on the telly.'

'But that's not *living* there, is it?'

'Anyway,' said Benny, anxious to get back to the dares. 'When are we ever going to have to swim in a shark-infested river?'

'We might,' said Tucker.

'Yeah, and our dog might play in goal for England.'

That was pretty conclusive. But Tucker was not going to lose out to anyone. Not in the daredevil stakes. He had something else up his sleeve.

'All right, Mastermind. I know *something* you wouldn't do.'

'What?'

Tucker looked secretive.

'Explore an ammunition dump.'

Benny was sceptical.

'What ammunition dump?'

Justin was fascinated.

'A *real* ammunition dump?'

'Yeah,' said Tucker. 'Well, it's old now, like. Our kid showed me last week. They used to make bombs and stuff there during the war.'

Justin: 'What do they do with it now?'

'Nothing,' said Tucker. 'It's abandoned.'

After that, Benny rubbished the idea. He couldn't see the point of it, if there weren't going to be bullets and stuff to be mucked about with. But Tucker was insistent. There *might* be something. A Second World War helmet or two, at least. Anyway, it would be a laugh. The clincher, of course, was that if Benny said no, Tucker would say he was scared. Blackmail.

For once, Benny would rather have ducked out. He had his new blazer on, and he remembered that morning, before school, when his Mum had given it to him. She'd been so proud and pleased that he wouldn't have to wear his old blue anorak any more, with all the other kids so smart. She'd called him Jim Dandy and been really happy. Such things meant a lot to parents, he knew. He didn't want to spoil that for her.

'I've got me new blazer on,' he said. 'My Mum'll kill me if I mess it up.'

Tucker's scorn was withering.

'Well *I'm* not wearing my pyjamas, am I?'

You can't win 'em all, thought Benny. Be nice to win just one or two, though. He gave in.

'All right,' he said. 'You're on.'

Justin was almost trembling. He was going to be so daring he might burst. He said simply: 'Can I come too?'

'No,' said Tucker. Just like that. No messing.

Justin gulped.

'Why not?'

'Why not?' asked Tucker. 'Why should we? *You* dropped us right in it in the swimming pool, remember?'

Justin felt bolder than he'd ever done before. He walked up to Jenkins and waved his chisel under his nose.

'Well, I'm sorry about that,' he said. 'But that was because you took my trousers.'

Tucker was quite taken aback. He'd never have believed weedy Bennett would even dream of raiding an ammunition dump. He consulted Benny.

'What do you reckon?'

Benny shrugged. Maybe the pale boy was human after all!

'OK by me,' he said.

So it was done. Tucker put on his Army- commander-over-the-top-men voice.

'Well that's it then, chaps! Operation Hevabutchers commences right after dinner! Roger?'

'Watch it!' hissed Benny. 'Here comes Parky.'

Three chisels flashed. Three rebates trembled.

Justin Bennett felt terrific.

77

It wasn't a long trek from school, and it was a nice sunny day to be out in. To Justin, from a distance, the old ammunition dump looked just like any derelict factory, with high brick walls and a tumbledown square chimney reaching up into the sky. But he didn't say anything. He was chuffed to death to be on an expedition with these two, and he wasn't going to spoil it.

The building was set back in its own grounds behind a high fence with barbed wire on top. But it was pretty old, and there were plenty of gaps low down in the wire mesh, hidden from the prying eyes of passers-by by overgrown bushes and stuff. They had no problem getting into the compound, and there was a lot of cover between the fence and the building.

Close to, the factory looked dangerous. All the glass was out of the windows, and some of the frames were hanging from the brickwork into the bargain; it appeared almost ready for demolition. Tucker pointed to a black hole in the side wall.

'There it is,' he said. 'We can get in through there.'

Justin hung back. Maybe being a daredevil didn't suit him after all!

'I've got my best shoes on,' he said.

And Benny mocked: 'I've got my *only* shoes on!'

'You're not backing out are you?' demanded Tucker. No. 'Well, come on, then!'

Once inside, Justin did not find it so bad. This was because the place stank so much, he forgot to be afraid. They weren't the first people who'd been there by a long shot – and most of the others had mistaken it for a public toilet. There was also the stink of rotting fabric, and something that reminded him of dead fish.

'Pooh,' he went. 'It doesn't half smell, doesn't it?'

Tucker, clambering over a pile of bricks, said: 'The only thing that smells in here is you, Justin my boy. You must've forgot to wash this morning!'

It was exciting at first, just being there. The place was big, and filthy, and littered with broken wood and bits of packing case. There were writings on the walls, and dirty drawings and stuff, and it echoed if you whooped. But it wasn't long before it began to be dead boring. They poked around all over, but there was no sign of anything to do with war. In fact there was no metal of any sort. Not even any old machinery.

'There's nothing here,' said Benny, finally.

'I can see that,' said Tucker. 'I'm not blind, you know.'

'I think we should go back,' said Justin, timidly. They ignored him.

'They must have left *something*,' said Tucker. 'Bullets are only small, you know.'

Benny was sarcastic.

'Just as well you've got a bionic eye then, isn't it.'

'Ha ha,' said Tucker Jenkins. 'I suppose you think that's funny.'

Benny pushed open a narrow wooden door, and they trooped into a small room with fuse boxes bolted to the walls.

'Not as funny as you thinking this place used to be an ammo dump. If you ask –'

With shocking suddenness, the door swung closed behind them. Tucker and Benny jumped a foot, and Justin nearly took off into orbit.

'What was that!' squeaked Ben.

Tucker put on a bold face. But he didn't sound so gutsy.

'Probably the wind,' he said.

'There wasn't any wind when we came in, Tucker.'

'Well, it must've star –'

There was a heavy crash outside their little prison, followed by an eerie wailing. It was like a lost soul. Like a banshee. Like a . . .

'It's a ghost!' breathed Justin, petrified. 'There's a ghost out there!'

In the normal way, Tucker and Benny would have fallen about. But today was different. Tucker reached into his inside jacket pocket and pulled a chisel out. He held it in front of him like a sword.

'What are you doing?' said Benny. 'Where'd you get that from?'

'I borrowed it from woodwork,' said Tucker. 'In case it came in handy.'

'Don't be stupid, Tucker,' said Benny. 'Put it away.'
Justin began almost to babble.

'We shouldn't have come,' he said. 'We should have gone back when I said to. This place is haunted. It's a ghost and –'

A horrible rustling noise came from outside the door. It was like footsteps in deep autumn leaves. Tucker brandished the chisel half-heartedly, then put it away as a bad job. Against a *ghost*? They all moved back as far as they could get in the tiny room. The rustling stopped.

'Look,' said Benny, after a minute's silence. 'Let's both try the door shall we, Tucker?'

'No!' said Justin.

Tucker hung back.

'Er. I . . . Why don't we wait a bit?' he said. 'It might go away.'

'I thought you were tougher than me,' said Benny. Oh no! thought Justin. Not dares! Not with death and destruction outside! But Tucker took the challenge.

'All right,' he said. 'I will if you will.'

Slowly, they approached the door. They both got a good grip on the edge and placed their feet where they would not slip. They glanced at each other, leaned back together, and nodded.

Crash! The door burst open and they shot out into the larger room. As they did so, a manky, mangy cat emerged from a pile of torn-up brown paper beside a packing case. It let out a squawk and raced away. Tucker, trying to save face, pretended not to have seen.

'Flipping heck!' he said. 'What was that!'

Benny said drily: 'A cat, stupid. That was the rustling. In that paper there. And the whining. Ours does that sometimes. It must have knocked that box over.'

'It sounded like a ghost to me,' said Justin. 'I was really scared.'

'Listen,' said Tucker, scornfully. 'No ghost could scare me. I was ready for anything.'

Benny flapped his elbows like wings and made a chicken noise.

'No!' said Tucker. 'I knew all along it was a cat, honestly. I was just waiting to see how long it'd be before you two realized!'

Benny merely whistled. Even Justin thought Tucker was pushing his luck a bit. He looked at his watch.

'Don't you think we should go now? We'll be late back if we're not careful.'

But Tucker had his eye on a rotting staircase.

'Nah, we haven't looked upstairs yet, have we? Come on, men, there's plenty of time.'

At last they'd found something worth having. In the upper part of the building there was an old trolley, the type with two wheels and a flat fork at the front, to carry boxes on. Tucker grabbed the handles and gave it an experimental shove. The wheels still worked.

'Get on, Benny!'

Benny needed no urging. He squatted on the forks and made engine and brake noises as Tucker raced him around. After half a circuit they locked in on Justin and exocetted him. Then they decided to be bull fighters. Justin got on the forks and stuck his arms out like horns, while Tucker got his blazer off to use as a matador's cape. Benny was the pusher, shoving and gasping as he made runs at El Jenkinso.

'Torro! Torro!' shouted Tucker. Each time Justin's horns got close he swept the blazer over his head and twirled away. Oh, very professional!

Benny got as far away as he could and prepared for his greatest charge. He pawed the filthy old floor with his hooves, while Justin made furious-bull roars. At a shout from Tucker they began to run.

When they were upon him, going flat out, Tucker neatly sidestepped, dropping his blazer over Benny's head. Benny, blinded, went careering on. He couldn't stop. There was a hole in the rotten planks, and Justin saw it coming. He gave a yell, the trolley crashed, and he ended up in a heap in the dirt. Luckily there was a layer of planking under the broken flooring. But he'd almost had enough.

What's more – he heard a noise. The squealing of brakes. Like a truck stopping. Then a door bang.

'Ssh!' he said. 'Listen!'

But Benny and Tucker were preparing for the next lark. They'd put the trolley back the right way up, and Benny had the handles. Tucker waved him onwards, imperiously.

'Forward, slave!'

'Please,' hissed Justin. 'Let's get out of here. I'm *sure* I heard something.'

Tucker laughed. But he went across to one of the window holes and poked his head out.

'Flipping heck!' he said. He pulled his head back hurriedly. His smile had gone. 'There's two blokes coming in the gate! Quick! Let's get out of here!'

The three of them were down the staircase like the wind. They began to make for the exit hole, but realized they would be cut off. Benny pointed to a pile of packing cases against a high wall. It led to the flat roof of an outhouse that overlooked the waste land outside. It was their only chance.

Tucker and Benny were much quicker than Justin, who hadn't had much practise at this sort of thing. Within half a minute they were on the roof. It was tarmac, and warm in the sunshine. There was a low parapet on the other side, the freedom side. They nipped across towards it, with rising hope. If there was a way down they could make it – easy. Justin, behind them, had reached the top of the wall. He was trying to pull himself over, wondering if he dared call to them to help. He did not think he would make it on his own.

Benny popped his head over the far side, with Tucker's just beside it in an instant. Ten feet below them was a man in overalls, looking up. So that was that.

'Right,' he said grimly. 'Back you go.'

And below Justin, another man roared: 'Oy!'

With only a little cry, Justin Bennett toppled backwards from the roof. When Tucker and Benny looked over, a second later, he was lying there, sprawled out on the ground. He looked like a broken doll, livid white. He looked dead.

The man bending over him turned a shocked face up to the boys.

'I think you'd better come down here,' he said.

Benny Green and Tucker Jenkins were left in the corridor outside the headmaster's room for what felt like eternity. They didn't know what was going on, they didn't know if Justin Bennett was a corpse, in hospital, or what. They just sat there, side by side, talking only every now and then. They both knew they were for it, this time, that they'd really done the business. To put the tin lid on it, Old Mitch had found the chisel in Tucker's pocket. You'd have thought it was a murder weapon.

One of the men who'd found them in the factory had turned up at the school, then – horror of horrors – Benny's Mum had come. Five minutes later it was Mrs Jenkins's turn. They'd both turned faces on their sons that were a cross between shame and fury, but neither had said a word. The corridor might have been death row.

Tucker said: 'Why do you think they've asked our Mums?'

Benny replied: 'Dunno. It could be to expel us.'

'Oh no! My dad would . . . on *no*!'

'Yeah,' said Benny. 'So would mine.'

The door opened and Mr Starling came out. The head. He had the factory man with him.

'Thank you, Mr Gregson,' he said gravely. 'You have been most understanding.'

The man stared hard at the boys. Remembering their faces. They both went hot.

'So long as it doesn't happen again,' he said. 'You two don't know how lucky you've been.'

The atmosphere of doom built up. The man walked down the passageway. The headmaster shook his head.

'I am talking to your mothers now,' he said. 'I will deal with you shortly.'

The boys heard about their punishment – and how Justin was – a good time later, after the grown-ups conference. They were ushered into the headmaster's room, and tried to avoid their mothers' eyes. They listened in silence as Justin's injuries were listed. A broken leg, severe concussion. And – Mr Starling considered it a matter of deepest shame – his father was likely to remove him from the school. Because of certain influences. It was not spelled out, but it was clear: because of boys like Peter Jenkins and Benjamin Green, Grange Hill was not good enough.

'There can be no point in going over what has happened,' he concluded. 'You both know exactly what you have been guilty of. I don't suppose you have anything to say?'

They shook their heads. Nothing to say.

'And I should think not. Which only leaves the question of suitable punishment,' said Mr Starling. 'A number of suggestions have been made. You, Green. You, for example, could be permanently suspended from the football team.' A look of horror crept over Benny's face. 'Or Jenkins. You could easily be barred from the school trip abroad.' Ouch, thought Tucker. 'However, the final form of punishment has been agreed with your parents. Indeed –it was upon their specific request.'

Both boys stole glances at their Mums from under their eyelashes. They waited.

'For the first time in the school's history as a comprehensive,' said Mr Starling. 'I am going to administer corporal punishment. And I hope it will be a lesson that neither of you will ever, *ever* forget.'

Mr Starling was a big man, and a powerful one. Forgetting a caning from him did not seem very likely. Both boys looked at their mothers, now. Tucker could hardly believe it. His Mum didn't even *approve* of that. She must be absolutely *wild* with him. Mrs Jenkins caught his look.

'You do well to look like that, my lad,' she said. 'But just you wait until your father hears about it.'

They were put outside again until the Mums had gone. Tucker tried to joke about it all, but by now his bravado was thin. Paper thin.

'How many do you think we'll get?' he asked. 'Six of the best?'

Benny did not reply. He was beyond idle chat.

'You've got to blow on your hands,' said Tucker. 'That's the way. It don't hurt so much then.' A worrying thought occurred. 'Unless we get it on the bum, of course.' Mm. 'How many can you take, d'you reckon?'

Benny only spoke to shut him up.

'Dunno,' he said. 'As many as you I suppose.'

'Rubbish,' said Tucker. 'I bet you can't.'

Benny thought his mate must be mental.

'Look shut up, Tucker,' he said. 'That's how you got us into this, isn't it? Betting and dares and crap. Don't you *ever* learn?'

Tucker tried to laugh, but his voice almost let him down. He was petrified. There was hardly any hiding it.

'I'm sorry, Ben,' he said. 'It's only . . . it's only because I'm scared, too.'

They smiled at each other in joint relief. The door to the headmaster's office opened, and Mr Mitchell stood there. He looked almost as sad as they did. He jerked his head.

'Come on, then,' he said.

They followed him inside.

CHAPTER SEVEN

Fighting Dirty

You lose one, you win one – that seemed to be the rule for One Alpha, even if it did not apply to Tucker and Benny. They lost one – and gained four each, across the hand, hard. Like the man said, they didn't forget it in a hurry.

One Alpha lost Justin Bennett, for a time at least, and possibly for good depending on how his father felt when it came to it. But the class gained a replacement called Michael Doyle. He was about the same size and shape as Justin, although he was fair instead of dark. But there all similarities ended. Completely.

Tucker and Benny first saw Michael Doyle after a bit of horseplay on the stairs. They'd been discussing the school elections, for which Tucker was hoping to get a nomination, when Trisha Yates, another candidate, came clattering down. As she passed, Tucker knocked her exercise books flying. Without a word, but with enormous force, she swung her briefcase at his head, almost braining him. She was a hard one, Trisha. He almost saw stars.

'Jenkins!' It was Mr Mitchell, at the bottom. And with him was Michael Doyle, smiling strangely. 'Jenkins,' repeated Mr Mitchell wearily. 'Can't you go *anywhere* without making a nuisance of yourself?'

Inside the art room, Trisha sat next to Judy Preston, and nudged her.

'Watch Old Mitch,' she whispered. 'That's his girlfriend, that Miss Mather. *Bet* you.'

The girls watched like hawks. Mr Mitchell certainly smiled in a friendly-friendly way at the art teacher, and she *was* quite good looking for her age. He introduced her to the new boy.

'Miss Mather,' said Old Mitch. 'This is Michael Doyle.'

'Oh yes, Michael. Weren't you recently in Mr Malcolm's class?'

Judy and Trisha exchanged grins. She had a dead peculiar voice, Miss Mather. She was from Belfast.

'Yes, Miss,' said Michael Doyle.

'Right,' said the art teacher. 'Well, go and find yourself a place. I'll see you later.'

She faced the class. Mr Mitchell was still beside her.

'Quiet, please,' she said. 'Today I want you to continue with the props for the school festival. Everybody collect your equipment and make a start, OK? I'll be around to see you shortly.'

As the children sorted themselves out, Mr Mitchell asked her how the festival arrangements were coming on. Miss Mather flashed him a warm smile.

'Oh very well,' she said. 'Far better than I expected. Oh, I've got one problem, the props for the school play. I need a pair of flintlocks. You know, antique pistols for the kids to use as models.'

'Tricky.'

'It is, yes. Anyway – what about Doyle?'

Mr Mitchell's face got serious.

'Not much to tell,' he said. 'He could be a bit of a problem I'm afraid. He and a couple of his friends were caught bullying, so Mrs Munroe decided to split them up.'

Miss Mather gave a rich laugh.

'And put them under your firm hand of authority!' she said.

'It's my fiendish neckhold!'

Michael Doyle, although he had not been assigned any work yet, decided to collect a paintbrush from the pots. On his way back to his table, he noticed Benny's – unattended. Michael's brush was tatty, Benny's was new. So he did a swap. Benny, as it happened, was returning to his table, and saw it.

'Oy,' he said. 'That's my brush! Give it back!'

Doyle sized him up. Tiny. He gave a supercilious smile and turned away. When Benny grabbed at him, he swung round and pushed him hard. Benny careered four feet into Tucker's painting arm.

'Flipping heck, Benny! Look what you're doing!'

'It wasn't me!' said Benny. 'It was him. He pushed me!'

Tucker and Doyle faced up to each other. They were the same size. Doyle was mocking Tucker with his grin.

'Did you push him?'

'I might have done. What you going to do about it?'

This was a red rag to a bull.

'You'll *see,*' said Tucker, happily. 'Just you –'

But Miss Mather stepped between them delicately. She sized the situation up in a flash.

'I think it's time we got you settled in, Michael,' she said. 'Whose is this brush?'

'Mine, Miss,' said Benny. And took it from the new boy's hand. Michael Doyle was too busy glaring at Tucker Jenkins to notice. It was the beginning of a hate affair. You could see it a mile off.

Tucker, as he went back to his desk, was rather pleased. He liked a challenge.

Michael Doyle, despite having been booted out of one class for his pains, clearly liked a challenge also. Back in the One Alpha form room after art, he was formally introduced by Mr Mitchell. When Doyle had been assigned a desk, the tutor waved a piece of paper above his head.

'Now,' he said. 'I finally have the full list of One Alpha candidates for the election of First Year Representative on the School Council. Quiet everyone.'

The class grew very attentive. In his new position, Michael Doyle bided his time.

'Right,' said Mr Mitchell. 'Well, there seem to be three *definite* candidates. Trisha Yates . . . Peter Jenkins . . . and Ann Wilson.' He looked at the paper. 'There are also three rather dubious nominations. Snoopy. The Six Million Dollar Man . . . and our budgie, because he can't half talk!'

There was a roar of approval for these three entrants, but Mr Mitchell put on a serious face.

'The final three will have to be disqualified,' he said. 'As none of them are actually members of the form! Now. Which of you, if any, would like to speak first?'

Trisha Yates looked uncomfortable. She'd been having second thoughts.

'Er. Before I speak, sir,' she said. 'Can I ask a question? Would I have to go to meetings and things? If I was elected?'

'Yes, you would,' he replied. 'About once a month, I think. Plus others as required if –'

'Oh,' said Trisha, hurriedly. 'In that case, sir, I'd . . . I'd rather not stand after all.'

Puzzled face from form tutor.

'Why is that?'

Tucker shouted coarsely: 'She can't stand the pace, sir!'

'Be quiet, Jenkins!'

'Well, sir,' said Trisha. 'It's just that . . . Well, I'm not the type for meetings and that, sir. I know I'd end up missing them. And then . . . well, I'd be letting everyone down, wouldn't I?'

Mr Mitchell was impressed. He complimented her on her 'honest and mature attitude'. Trisha nearly died. Then Ann Wilson, tall, self-contained and sensible, put her hand up. Mr Mitchell nodded, and she spoke. But first, she took a very deep breath.

'This may not sound very nice, sir,' she said quietly. 'But I don't think Peter Jenkins should be nominated.'

Tucker was furious. He jumped to his feet, shouting:

'Why not! I've got just as much right as you!'

Half the class was for him, half for Ann. It began to turn into a slanging match. Mr Mitchell banged his desk lid to bring them back to order. When they were quieter, he called on Ann to explain herself.

'Well, sir,' she said. 'What I mean is . . . well, if I'm nominated, and elected, I'll do my best, sir. For everyone. But he's . . . well . . . he just messes about all the time, sir. He never takes anything seriously and . . . oh, you know what I mean.'

'*I* do,' said Trisha staunchly. 'He's horrible!'

'*I'm* not horrible,' yelled Tucker. 'If anyone's horrible round here it's you, Pongo!'

'Oh shut up, Jenkins,' retorted Trisha. 'Ann's entitled to her opinion.'

'It's a *stupid* opinion.'

Judy Preston was getting steamed up. She was bouncing around in her seat like a kettle boiling.

'No it's not! You're the one who's stupid,' she said. 'We don't want someone who always gets the cane!'

'That was *once,*' said Tucker, in disgust.

Trisha said: 'Once was enough.'

And Judy added: 'No one else has *ever* had it!'

Mr Mitchell decided to take a hand. This was getting like a *real* election! Dirty.

'Look,' he said. 'You're all obviously entitled to your own opinions, but the rights and wrongs of Mr Jenkins receiving corporal punishment is not the issue here. All you have to do is decide whether or not he would make a good representative and promote our interests.'

Tucker blew a loud raspberry.

'Right!' said Mr Mitchell. 'Thank you, Jenkins. Down here where I can keep an eye on you!'

'Oh, sir!'

'Jenkins! Come on! Jump to it!' Tucker sauntered out front. 'Run!' He speeded up to a snail's pace. 'That's running? Thank you. Now. Anybody else want to speak?'

To everybody's surprise, the new boy stuck his hand up.

'I'd like to put myself forward as a candidate, sir,' he said.

The cheek of the bloke!

'Oh,' said Mr Mitchell. 'Well, Doyle. Well, you weren't here yesterday, were you? So I think we *can* accept your nomination. Have you anything to say for yourself?'

Michael Doyle did not suffer from shyness or false modesty. He said: 'Only that I'm the best man for the job, sir.' He appeared to believe it, too. There was a chorus of groans from the rest of One Alpha.

'Oh. And why do you say that?'

'Because my Dad's a councillor, sir, so I know all about –'

Tucker, standing against the wall out front, mimicked: 'My Dad's a councillor! So I know blablahblah!'

Benny shouted: 'My Mum says all the council should be shot. They keep putting up the rent!'

Michael Doyle looked at him venomously.

'Then your Mum's *stupid*, isn't she?'

It was pretty clear from the class's response to *that*, that Michael Doyle had no chance. Nor had Tucker, as it happened. The winner, by a landslide, was Ann Wilson – with one vote for the disqualified budgie.

'Somehow,' said Mr Mitchell, 'I don't think the ability to stand on one leg and say 'Who's a pretty boy then' would be of much use on the School Council.'

A grin flashed across his face.

'Oh. I don't know though . . .'

If Michael Doyle couldn't get a nomination, that didn't mean he couldn't play a part. At break, he went back towards his old classroom and found his mate, David Robinson. Robinson, a small dark boy, was one of the trio who had been split up for bullying. And Robinson – by a fluke, or bribery and corruption – had got the nomination for his form. Michael Doyle immediately appointed himself campaign manager. This, he thought, would be a walkover.

'How much money have you got?' he asked. 'We've got to buy more sweets than anybody else to dish around. That's the way to do it.' He grinned. 'And we can always bash a few of the little'uns,' he said. 'I know half a dozen votes we can get before we start.'

Robbo Robinson made a Chinese burn gesture with his hands.

'Yeah,' he said. 'Hey, Mickey. It should be a good laugh, this.'

Ann Wilson's campaign, naturally, was all fair and above board. She took on Judy Preston as her campaign manager, with Trisha and little Mary as helpers. The first thing to do, they decided, was design a poster. When they found it wasn't easy to make one look good, they didn't panic. They went to Mr Mitchell. And Mr Mitchell, who secretly hoped that Ann would win, took them to see Miss Mather – much to the delight of Trisha and Judy. They might pick up some scandal!

'Er . . . you're not busy, are you?' he asked, poking his head around the art room door.

'No,' laughed Miss Mather. 'But I've got a sneaking suspicion I will be in a minute!'

'Well actually, it's not for me. It's for these young ladies here. They're trying to design a poster for the election. Ann here's been nominated for our form.'

'Good for you, Ann!' said Miss Mather. 'Now – let's have a look at it.'

The poster was plain and rather messy. It said simply: Vote for Ann Wilson. Not very eye-catching, they all agreed.

'Right,' said Miss Mather. 'Come on, girls. Let's see what we can do.'

Mr Mitchell left them to it with a nod. Trisha and Judy were vaguely disappointed. He didn't even blow a kiss!

The candidate for Alan Hargreaves' class, K1, was a boy called Adrian Jones. Alan reckoned on getting Tucker's vote on the old pal's act if nothing else. But he told Adrian beforehand that a sweet or two might help. They ran Tucker and Benny to earth at the bottom of a stairwell towards the end of the dinner break.

'Go on, Tucker,' urged Alan. 'If you vote for him we'll all get what we want.'

'From what you say,' Adrian added, 'I stand for most of the things you want in any case.'

Tucker gave him a crafty look.

'I'll tell you what I'll do,' he said. 'Give me a sweet and I will . . .' Adrian, looking sour, gave him one. '. . . *think* about it!' said Tucker.

'Huh,' went Adrian. He turned to Benny. 'What about you?'

Benny was not a bargainer. He just like sweets.

'Yeah,' he said. 'I'll vote for you. If you give me a sweet.'

So that was easily settled. Alan and Adrian left, with one definite and one possible. A fair percentage . . .

Almost immediately, Trisha, Ann and Judy turned up.

'Watch out,' said Tucker loudly. 'It's the three little pigs.'

'Were you talking to Adrian Jones just now?' accused Trisha.

'So what if we were?'

'Are you going to vote for him?'

'I might. He gave me a sweet. *She's* never given me any sweets, has she?'

Ann pulled a face. She did *not* approve of bribery.

Tucker went on: 'Anyway, that Adrian bloke seemed a bit of a bright spark to me.'

Trisha, who had no idea about vote-catching, let's face it, retorted: 'Anyone would be a bright spark next to you!'

Tucker sneered. Benny chipped in with: 'He is a bright spark. He wants to abolish cricket.'

Ann raised her eyebrows.

'And that's the only reason you'll vote for him!'

'The *only* reason?! We have Frosty Foster. It's all right for you lot,' said Tucker.

'But you *can't,*' insisted Judy. 'You'd be letting the form down!'

'All right, then,' said Benny, to calm Judy Preston down. 'What's her policy?'

Ann squared her shoulders.

'I'm going to support the campaign to abolish the school uniform,' she said.

Benny squawked with laughter. He lifted his leg up and waggled it. Under his smart blazer his jeans looked even scruffier than before.

'That settles it then!' he said. 'You've lost *my* vote! I've already abolished half my uniform!'

Michael Doyle and David Robinson did most of their electioneering in secret corners and with muttered threats or offers, so to Ann and Co. it was Jones who seemed to be their real rival. Doyle did tear a few posters down, but that did not worry them a lot. What did was the number of votes that weren't committed to the uniform cause. The first excitement soon died away, and the campaign took on the grinding aspect of real work. At one stage, Ann decided they needed some advice. They found Mr Mitchell alone in the classroom.

'Hello,' he said. 'Why all the glum faces?'

Judy said: 'We've been round asking everyone how they're going to vote.'

'Not good news, then?'

'No, sir. Most of the girls are behind Ann – mainly because she's the only girl candidate. But most of the boys are supporting that stupid boy from K1.'

'He wants to ban *cricket,*' said Trisha.

Ann said: 'It's all so silly, sir. A first-year isn't going to be able to change the timetable, is he, sir?'

Mr Mitchell did not commit himself.

'Can't you explain that to them, sir?' asked Trisha. 'Can't you tell them to vote for Ann?'

'Ah – that's your job,' he replied. 'Mine is to stay impartial.'

'Well it all seems such a waste of time, sir,' said Ann. 'All the boys are concerned about is not liking that horrible Mr Foster, sir– Oh! Oh, I'm sorry, sir!'

Mr Mitchell woggled his finger in his ear, suddenly deaf. He asked Ann exactly what she was offering as a draw.

'I'm supporting the abolition of the school uniform, sir,' she said.

'Yes, well,' he said dubiously. 'Quite frankly, Ann, half the boys in this school wouldn't notice if their trousers only had one leg. Don't you think you ought to offer something they'd *really* like. Or *appear* to, at least? That's how it's done, you know. Like, for instance . . . abolishing' (he winked) 'certain members of the sports staff, say!'

They could see what he was driving at. But *what* could they offer?

'What I suggest,' said Mr Mitchell, 'is that you go straight to the horse's mouth. Go out and talk to the boys, direct. And ask *them* what they want. Got it?'

They left Mr Mitchell with a new sense of urgency and purpose. They did not travel as a team any more, they went their separate ways. When they met up again a couple of hours later, they all had similar stories to tell about how horrible the boys were – all the boys. But they also had a new idea. For two things had emerged quite

clearly from their straw-poll. The first desire on the boys'
list was that they should push off – and the second was for
a school tuckshop.

Ann, Trisha, Judy and Mary streamed into the art room
and told Miss Mather. She was delighted, and impressed.

'What a super idea, Ann!' she said. 'It's a wonder no
one has ever thought of it before!'

Ann felt confident enough to share a joke with the
teacher.

'It's like all brilliant ideas, Miss,' she said. 'Simple but
effective! It was Mr Mitchell's really, though.'

Trisha and Judy nudged each other but, dis-
appointingly, Miss Mather did not faint at the mention of
his name. She did smile, though, when he entered the
room some time later. Because the first of the new posters
was ready – and it looked terrific.

VOTE
Wilson
VOTE
Tuckshop

'We're going to cover the school,' said Trisha Yates.
'We're going to put them everywhere!'

'You'll drive poor Mr Garfield mad,' laughed Mr
Mitchell.

Trisha was as good as her word. She had no fear, she had
no shame. She stuck the posters everywhere, in the
staffroom, on the outside noticeboard, on the hood of Mr
Mitchell's sports car, on the door of the boys' lavatories.
Mr Mitchell and Mr Malcolm, one breaktime, saw Trisha,
Mary and Ann actually knock one boy down, accidentally
on purpose, then cluster round him to help him pick up his
things. When he walked away there was a poster stuck
neatly to the back of his blazer. He was a walking advert
for Ann Wilson and her plan.

The campaign took off really well. Judy Preston wrote
an article in the magazine in which Ann was 'hotly tipped'
to win (by her!), and dozens of people stopped Ann round

the school to talk about it. She began to feel not only fairly confident, but fairly anxious. From being something that did not really matter, it became a real issue with her. She'd caught election fever!

On the day the votes were cast and counted, the whole school gathered in the hall. Mrs Munroe was the chief returning officer, with Mr Malcolm as her deputy. The other teachers were scattered round the hall to keep an eye on things.

But none of them noticed the 'fringe activities' of Michael Doyle and his candidate. They spent the voting time tracking down and pouncing on boys they'd already terrorised, making sure. Towards the end of voting, they tried a new victim. A small, blond boy they did not know. They pulled him into the corridor. Doyle bent his fingers back, and Robbo twisted his arm.

'Who you going to vote for? *Him*?'

'No I'm not. It's a secret and I'm – Aaagh!'

When they'd hurt him sufficiently, he promised. They pushed him back into the hall. Once there, he turned defiantly. 'I'm not telling you who I'm voting for,' he said. 'But it won't be you!'

At last Mrs Munroe called for order. She apologised for keeping them all waiting. But the results, she said, had been extremely close. Ann Wilson was dying of excitement. The first year result was coming first.

When the vote for Ann was announced, the excitement increased. She had forty four. Trisha, who had taken the last straw-poll, did frantic calculations.

'Andrew Cox, Form R1,' said Mrs Munroe. 'Nineteen votes.'

'I think we can do it,' hissed Trisha. 'Oh I *wish* we'd thought of the tuckshop earlier!'

'Malcolm Smith, Form N1, *three* votes.'

A ripple of laughter.

'It's this next one I'm worried about,' said Trisha. 'It's Adrian Jones.'

She need not have. Although Mrs Munroe read it first as forty seven votes for Adrian, it was Mr Malcolm's writing. He had forty one. Trisha did a quick count up. The awful truth began to dawn.

'Oh *no!*' she breathed.

Oh yes. Mrs Munroe read out the last name.

'David Robinson, Form G1. Forty *five* votes,' she said. 'So David Robinson is duly elected first form representative. Well done.'

Ann Wilson had never felt so disappointed in her life. Nor had her friends. To lose by one vote was awful enough. But David *Robinson!* It was terrible. With long faces they began to leave the hall.

'Now,' said Mrs Munroe. 'The second year figures. First . . .'

The small blond boy went to Mr Mitchell and whispered in his ear. Mr Mitchell looked shocked, then thoughtful.

'Ann,' he called. 'Don't leave. Just wait there.'

'Why, sir?' she asked miserably.

'Just *wait,*' he said. Michael Doyle and David Robinson, watching this, began to shift uncomfortably in their shoes.

The hall became quite noisy as the teachers on the platform went into a huddle. But there was dead silence as Mrs Munroe, her face grim, made her announcement. There had been coercion, she said, and bullying. It was a serious matter which would be dealt with most severely. But there would *not* be a re-election.

'What we have decided,' she said, 'is to disqualify the votes of the two boys concerned. David Robinson, therefore, now has forty three votes, not forty five. And Ann Wilson, with forty four, is the elected representative.'

Ann gasped. Trisha jumped three feet in the air, cheering. Mary and Judy slapped each other on the back. Michael Doyle and David Robinson started sneaking from the hall. But Mr Malcolm stopped them, and turned their faces to the platform.

'David Robinson,' said Mrs Munroe. 'And Michael Doyle. You will see me in my room immediately after afternoon registration. Immediately.'

She dismissed them with contempt.

'Now,' she said. 'The second year.'

Doyle and Robinson slunk out.

CHAPTER EIGHT

Pistols at Dawn

It said a lot for Michael Doyle's unpopularity with One Alpha that there was not one single person in the class who felt the slightest bit sorry for him. Tucker Jenkins was not just indifferent, he was cockahoop. He hated Michael Doyle, and figured they were at war – official. Round One had definitely not gone to Doyle. Round Two was a lot more personal, though. And more violent.

It started almost by an accident one morning when they were heading off to Miss Mather's class in the Art Room. Tucker and Benny, being early, had sneaked into the caretaker's basement junk room to have a mess around. Only because the door was open, naturally . . . Tucker was playing with a cylinder vacuum cleaner, while Benny – for reasons known only to himself – hung upside down from a ceiling fixture.

'Hey Tucker,' he called. 'What's this supposed to be then?'

Tucker regarded the upside down figure, which was now flapping its arms about.

'Dunno,' he said. 'Looks like a nut job hanging upside down on a coatrack.'

'No, you know what I mean! Who am I supposed to be?'

'Dunno,' repeated Tucker, fiddling with the cleaner. Suddenly, it began to hum.

'Batman!' shouted Benny. Then let out a roar as Tucker pointed the nozzle at him. It was blowing clouds of dust all over his sweater!

'Pack it in, Tucker!' he yelled.

Tucker tried to stop. The cleaner had gone crazy.

'Sorry, Benny,' he said. 'I'll try to get it off.'

Benny flipped over and dropped to the ground. As Tucker started to run, he picked up an old mophead and gave chase. At the first throw, it missed. Tucker darted up the stairway to ground level. Benny, haring after him, picked up the mophead and flung it once more. It bounced off Tucker's shoulder.

Whooping and laughing, they raced down the corridor towards the Art Room. Halfway along, Tucker spotted Doyle. He gripped his shoulder and spun him round, to use him as a shield. The mophead caught him in the face and left him spluttering. By the time Doyle had recovered, Benny was past, following Tucker into the class.

Michael Doyle was wild. Although it was too late, he was determined to retaliate. He stood in the entrance and checked that Miss Mather's back was turned. He buzzed the mophead hard across the room, towards Benny's un-suspecting head.

Bad shot. *Terrible* shot. The mophead landed on a drying piece of artwork. It smudged right across, yellow, green and red.

She was an easy-going teacher, Miss Mather. But when she saw the damage, her face went dark with anger.

'Who?' she said. 'Was responsible for *this!*'

Doyle, trapped, said lamely: 'I couldn't help it, Miss. He –'

'Do you *realise* how many people have worked on that? How much time and *effort* have gone into it? Just to be destroyed by your GROSS stupidity!?'

The normally-calm Miss Mather was trembling with rage. Doyle pointed feebly at Benny.

'It wasn't my fault, Miss. I was –'

'DID you throw it?'

'Only cause he –'

'DID YOU THROW IT!'

Doyle gave up. He flashed a look of hate at Benny. And admitted it.

'Very well,' said Miss Mather, beginning to get her self-control screwed back into place. 'You will meet me at Mrs Munroe's office at break. Is that clear?'

Oh, Gawd, thought Doyle. Not Mrs Munroe again!

'But I was –'

'DOYLE! DISAPPEAR!'

He walked past her, scuffing his heels. The rest of the class were crowded in the doorway, goggle-eyed.

'All right,' said Miss Mather. 'The show's over. Get to your places.'

As Doyle walked past Benny he muttered: 'I'll get you for that, Golly.'

Trisha Yates was last in, and she walked into trouble. She was wearing coloured tights, and not just single-coloured, either. They were in garish horizontal bands, red and blue. *Very* smart. Miss Mather said icily: 'Well?'

'Well what, Miss?'

The famous self-control was rapidly coming unstuck again.

'I am in no mood for guessing games, Trisha. What's the school uniform?'

'White socks, Miss.'

'White socks, Trisha. Are you colour blind?' No, went Trisha's head. 'Then why in heaven's *name* are you wearing *those?*' There was no answer. And a pause. Miss Mather said: 'Perhaps three hours detention will refresh your memory.'

'Three *hours!*' gasped Trisha Yates. 'But that's not fair! You wear them!'

It was the wrong thing to say. The class watched, with baited breath. Miss Mather took several deep breaths.

'*I* am not in the first form,' she said at last. 'I *happen* to be a member of *staff*. Or hadn't you *noticed!*' Trisha stared at the floor. 'Now go and sit down,' said Miss Mather. 'Just go and sit down.'

She stood in front of the class for quite some time before she trusted herself to sound normal. Sometimes, she thought, I hate the little swines. She looked sideways to where a pair of antique pistols lay, on polished cradles. She almost regretted the effort she'd put in on their behalf.

'Right,' she said. 'Today we're going to carry on with the props for the festival. To help you, I've managed to borrow those for you to use as models.' She gestured at the pistols. 'But I must emphasise, that *great care* must be taken with them at all times. At . . . all . . . times. Is that clear?'

'Right,' said Miss Mather. She could feel herself re-
laxing. 'Get your gear out, then.'

In the mêlée, Michael Doyle came forward and touched
one of the pistols. In his head, a neat revenge was forming.
Miss Mather checked him, but not unpleasantly.

'Careful, Doyle,' she said. 'We don't want any more
damage done. Do we?'

Michael Doyle engaged the help of David Robinson when
he stole one of the pistols. They waited in the corridor in
the lunch hour until Miss Mather left the Art Room. She
was only going for a minute or two, so she did not bother to
lock it. Robbo kept watch while Doyle wrapped the antique in a piece of brown paper.

It took less than half a minute, and if they had not run,
nobody would ever have known it was them, in all prob-
ability. But they did run. Tucker, who was by the lockers in
the corridor, watched them in surprise, although they did
not notice him. He wondered idly what they'd been playing
at.

It was mid-afternoon before news of the theft arrived at
Alpha One, and it arrived with the rather forbidding figure
of Mrs Munroe, who opened the classroom door and asked
if she might speak to Mr Mitchell outside. When he returned, his face was serious. The class listened more intently than usual as he outlined what had happened. One of
the pistols had gone, and the headmaster was incensed.
Because of the timing of the disappearance, suspicion had
to fall on One Alpha and only one other class. And if the
pistol was not found . . . the consequences would be
serious.

Prompted by Ann Wilson, he listed those consequences.
Mr Starling, he said, was threatening to cancel the school
festival – all of it, lock, stock and barrel. If the thought of
that did not prompt somebody to own up, the police would
be called in. And the unpleasantness would start in earnest.

'What I would like to ask,' he concluded, as the bell
began to ring, 'is this: if anyone knows anything, anything
at all, about this – come and tell me. It won't go any further,

I promise. Or, if you prefer, you can write it on a piece of paper and leave it in my rack outside the staffroom. OK? Right. You'd better go.'

The class trooped out quietly, almost decorously. But as Trisha made to leave, Mr Mitchell called her over. She knew immediately what it was.

'I understand from Mrs Munroe,' he said sternly, 'that Miss Mather has given you a three-hour detention for failing to comply with the school uniform. And before that, it was Miss Clarke, for wearing earrings.' Mr Mitchell, who was normally pretty friendly, sounded cold, and distant. Trisha felt bad.

'I'm not interested, Trisha, in explanations or excuses,' he went on. 'I'm just warning you that it can't go on. Do you understand?'

She felt a jerk, giving him extra little things to worry about when he had something serious on his plate. She hung her head.

'Yes sir,' she said. 'I'm sorry, sir. It won't happen again.'

'Won't it?' he said, rather wearily. 'Ah well, just see that it doesn't. OK?'

She nodded. Guiltily. And left.

Tucker Jenkins, thoughtful, waited on the stairs while the others trooped down past him. Doyle, who had nothing to do with any of the others, came alone. Tucker stepped deliberately into his path.

'You're in my way,' said Doyle. 'Move.'

'You took that gun,' said Tucker.

Michael Doyle gave Jenkins a look of total contempt.

'What if I did?' he said. 'What are you going to do about it?'

Cool swine, thought Tucker Jenkins.

'Tell Mr Mitchell,' he said flatly.

Doyle smiled.

'Tell him what, though?'

'Tell him I seen you running away from the Art Room.'

Doyle didn't even appear shaken.

'So what?' he said. 'That proves nothing. It's only your word against mine. And *my* Dad's a councillor.'

He jostled Tucker to one side and clattered on downwards. Benny, who'd been sorting out some sports gear, joined his mate.

'What was all that about?'

They started to descend together. Trisha Yates, released by Mr Mitchell, came down behind them, unnoticed. Her ears pricked up, and she listened to their conversation. Interesting, she thought. *Very* interesting.

Further ahead, along the bottom corridor, Ann Wilson and Mary were getting their first taste of ostracism. Some third year girls ganged up on them.

'Hey, wait a minute,' said one of them. 'Aren't you in One Alpha?'

'Yeah,' said Mary, as Trisha jogged up and joined them. 'Why? What do you want?'

The third year poked Mary in the chest.

'I'll tell you what we want,' she said. 'We want the festival to take place.'

'So do we!' said Ann.

'We've put a lot of time and effort into it,' the girl continued.

'So have we,' said Mary.

The older girl poked her again.

'I'm supposed to be *in* it!' she snapped. 'And I can't risk having it cancelled.'

Trisha was getting dead humpy.

'*We* didn't take that flintlock,' she said angrily.

The situation was getting ugly. Another third year put her hand on the girl's sleeve.

'Oh come on, Janet,' she said. 'You can't do any good like that.'

If looks could have withered, Ann and Mary and Trisha would have had it. The girl stabbed a finger at them as she was dragged away.

'Just you remember. Got it?'

The three of them were left feeling rather shaken.

'Phew,' said Ann. 'News certainly travels fast in this place, doesn't it?'

'Yeah,' said Mary. 'Horrible. It's not fair, why pick on us? It's not our fault.'

Trisha remembered her news. She gabbled out what she had overheard. Even though it was Tucker Jenkins – who was *not* to be relied on – Ann and Mary agreed it was worth checking on.

'I'm *sure* there's something in it,' Trisha said. 'I don't trust that Doyle. His eyes are too close together.'

Mary's jaw dropped.

'I never noticed that!' she said.

The thing they had to do was track down Jenkins and interrogate. That wouldn't be too difficult. During spare time in the school, he and Benny practically *lived* in the cloakroom. It was a second home to them.

Sure enough the boys were in among the coats, breaking the school rules with a quiet card game. When the girls appeared, Tucker said in a tone of disgust: 'What do *you* lot want?'

Trisha, automatically, replied: 'You're a pig, you are.'

'Takes one to know one, Porky.'

The social niceties over, Ann asked Tucker: 'Did you see that Doyle hanging around the Art Room?'

He was surprised. 'Who says that?' he asked.

'I did,' said Trisha. 'I heard you tell Benny Green that –'

'Trisha,' said Ann firmly. 'Let me.' To Jenkins: '*Did* you?'

Tucker eyed her up and down. She was all right, Ann Wilson, you could trust her. Posh but straight.

'Yeah,' he said. 'And he practically told me. *He* whizzed that gun.'

Mary said: 'Why didn't you tell Mr Mitchell?'

'Because I can't prove it, can I? It'd only be my word against his. But he did it. No question.'

'Why are you so sure?' asked Ann, fair to the last. Benny answered scornfully.

'Because he got told off by that Miss Mather.'

'So did Trisha,' Ann replied. 'But *she* didn't steal anything.'

Tucker hooted.

'How do *we* know!' And got kicked by Trisha for his

104

pains. He grinned. 'Only joking,' he said. There was serious business under way.

'Anyway,' continued Benny. 'Trisha didn't get sent to Mrs Munroe and banned from the festival, did she?'

Mary was shocked.

'Is that what happened to him?'

'Yeah,' said Tucker. 'And he got ten hours detention, too. It wasn't just the picture he mucked up, was it? It come on top of that election stuff as well. He's in lumber, that kid. I'm glad to say.'

'So he could have done it to get his own back, couldn't he?' said Benny.

Ann nodded.

'It's only an idea though. I mean, we couldn't prove it, could we?'

Tucker was getting impatient.

'We could if we grabbed him and *made* him talk.'

'That's *bullying*,' said Ann. 'And anyway, what would happen if he told Mr Mitchell? Or Mrs Munroe?'

Tucker flexed his muscles.

'He won't tell anyone anything by the time I'm finished with him.'

'Yah,' went Trisha. 'You couldn't punch a hole in a wet paper bag.'

'I'll punch you in a minute, Pongo!'

Mary intervened to keep the peace.

'We could send him to Coventry,' she suggested. 'To let him know we know it was him.'

'We *don't* know!' said Ann. But no one was on her side over that one. They were convinced.

'Anyway,' said Benny. 'It wouldn't do any *harm*, would it? I mean, he's not a very *nice* geezer, is he?'

Mary smirked, taking the mickey out of Trisha.

'No,' she said. 'His eyes are too close together!'

Ann was so near being certain that she nagged just a little more. 'Are you *sure* you saw him acting suspiciously?' she asked.

'Yes,' said Jenkins, seriously. 'I said so, didn't I?'

Ann's face relaxed. She brushed her hair back from her eyes.

105

'Yes!' she said. 'And you also told everyone the headmaster had a wooden leg!' Smiles all round. Ann had made her mind up. 'Anyway,' she continued, 'I don't suppose it would do any harm just to pressurise Doyle a *little* bit, would it?'

Tucker went into a Kojak routine, bending at the waist and brandishing a pretend lollipop.

'Right on, sweetheart!' he said, in a cool American accent. 'Let's go, Benny-baby. Time to put the frighteners on the dude! Wha' d'ya say!'

Benny did a Kojak walk as well, and the pair of them made for the door like loonies.

'Ah'm with ya, man!' said Benny.

'Who loves ya, baby!'

The girls were left shaking their heads.

Say what you like about Doyle – and people did, people did! – he was no pushover. It took him some time to realise he was the victim of a campaign, but when he'd worked it out he did not let it get to him.

The first move, inevitably, came from Tucker Jenkins. Shortly after the meeting with the girls, he and Benny turned the corner into a corridor and saw their prey in front of them. Alone. They soft-shoed up behind him until they were within striking range, then put on a spurt.

'Banzai!' Tucker yelled, flying through the air at Doyle's back. Doyle half turned, too late. The pair of them knocked him flying and ran on. Tucker shouted back at him: 'Sorry, Doyly! I mistook you for the feller that whizzed that gun!'

The girls were more subtle, but equally brutal in their own way. In the Art Room one morning, for example, Doyle moved up to Trisha's table and asked politely if he could borrow a pencil. She did not even glance up.

'Sorry.'

'There's one there,' said Michael Doyle, pointing across her table. Trisha picked it up. She put down the pencil she had been working with.

'I'm using it.'

Judy Preston, overhearing, leaned backwards in her seat and said sweetly: 'Can I borrow a pencil, Trisha?'

Trisha turned and smiled.

'Sure,' she said, and gave her one.

Doyle stared at her, then glared at her.

'Why didn't you lend it to me?'

Trisha met his eyes, coolly.

'I don't lend things to certain types of people,' she said. 'I might not get them back.'

It wasn't long before the whole class was involved. Coming out for morning break one day, Doyle walked into an ambush. Hughes and Underwood tripped him up, and little Tommy Watson pushed him over. Other boys came out and stood there laughing at him. When Doyle had sorted himself out, Tucker Jenkins was among the crowd. Without a word, Doyle jumped for him. The crowd was soon roaring encouragement.

Mr Mitchell broke it up, and demanded to know what was going on.

'Ask him,' said Tucker Jenkins. 'He knows.'

But Doyle was not saying. At four o'clock the pair of them were hauled in front of Mitchell and asked again. They accepted their hour's detention apiece stoically. Doyle's smile spoke volumes to Tucker. It said: 'You won't break me, Jenkins. No way.'

When Tucker walked into the cloakroom some days later to rendezvous with Benny, Ann, Judy and Trisha were already there.

'What do you lot want?' he asked, chucking a sweet to Benny, who was looking at a football mag.

'They want to talk about Doyle the Boil,' said Benny.

'What about him?'

Judy Preston said: 'It's been ages since we sent him to Coventry, and it doesn't look like he's *ever* going to own up.'

'We've got to think of something else,' said Trisha.

Ann sat down tiredly among the coats. 'If you ask me,' she said, 'he didn't take the flintlock after all.'

'*Course* he did!' said Tucker. Judy pulled a face.

107

'Then why won't he own up?'

'You're thick, you are,' Tucker replied. 'He isn't going to own up if it means he'll get the bullet, is he?'

'What do you mean?' said Judy, who wasn't quite sure what 'the bullet' was.

'Look,' said Tucker. 'If he takes the flintlock back it'll be just like saying . . .' (He put on a squeaky girl's voice) '. . . please sir, I whizzed that gun! Would you like to expel me or hand me over to Old Bill?'

'Old Bill?' said Judy. 'Who's Old Bill?'

'Oh Judy!' said Trisha. Ann Wilson was looking thoughtful.

'If that's the case, Tucker,' she said, 'what we've got to do is work out some way of making sure that Doyle – or *whoever* it was – won't get into trouble if it's returned.'

Benny was startled. He believed that criminals should be made to pay.

'What's the point of *that*?'

Judy said: 'Well at least the festival would take place, wouldn't it? Oh Ann, how –'

'I still think we should *make* him confess,' said Benny.

'So do I,' said Trisha. Tucker did not even need to speak.

But Ann had a brainwave coming. You could see it in her face.

Ann went straightway to the classroom, and found Mr Mitchell talking to Mrs Munroe. She outlined her idea rather breathlessly to both of them. If the reason the pistol had not been returned was fear of the consequences – why not allow it to be given back anonymously? With no comeback. The 'criminal' would get away with it, true – but it did seem so unfair that the whole school was to be punished. And think of all the effort that everyone had put into the festival – pupils *and* staff. It would all be simply wasted.

Mr Munroe was impressed. But she was also dubious that the headmaster would wear it. But she'd try, she said. She certainly would try. She would go and see him right away . . .

That very afternoon, after registration, Mr Mitchell made the announcement. Mr Starling had agreed to give Ann's amnesty a chance, he said. Provided the flintlock was returned before 4 o'clock the following afternoon, no more would be said about it. But if it was not – that was that. The police were coming in to sort out the whole sorry business. He sent them off to take their next lesson, and he smiled at Ann as she went past.

'Fingers crossed, eh, Ann?' he said, suiting the action to the words. 'Fingers crossed!'

Benny, outside the form room, said to Tucker: 'It's not right, Tucker, is it? We all know Doyly took it. It's not right he should get away with it.'

'He won't,' said Tucker, enigmatically.

'What d'you mean? You heard what Mitchell said.'

'Yeah,' said Tucker. 'Come on. We've got work to do.'

At the end of school that day, Tucker and Benny lay in wait in one of the cloakrooms that let onto the yard. It was a route they knew Doyle took, and sure enough, after a couple of minutes they saw him sauntering along with David Robinson. What Tucker and Benny did not see, as they ducked behind the door, was two more of Doyle's mates some way behind, playing with a ball. At the right moment, Tucker pushed open the door and confronted the enemy. The enemy, unafraid, moved into the room.

'What do you want?' he said.

'We know you took that gun,' said Benny Green. Doyle sneered at him.

'I'm not talking to you, Golly,' he said. 'I haven't forgot that mop business yet. I'll sort you out for that.'

'The only thing you'll sort out,' put in Tucker, 'is how to get that gun back, got it?'

'Oh yeah. And who's going to make me?'

'We are.' Tucker took a fighting stance. Doyle laughed.

'Just the two of you?' he said. His mates appeared behind him, in the doorway. 'Against four of us!'

Tucker had been waiting for something like this. With a look of sheer pleasure he put his fingers in his mouth and whistled. The smile was wiped off Doyle's face as Alan

Hargreaves emerged from a lavatory cubicle. Alan was fat. And big. And strong. He ambled forward.

'That's still only three, Jenkins,' said Michael Doyle bravely. Tucker whistled once more, and another cubicle opened. Tucker's face said it all.

Quick as a flash, Doyle's mates turned and ran. As they sped round the corner of the building, Tucker and his lot pulled Doyle down. Grimly, they frog-marched him to the back of the cloakroom. Silent, but struggling.

Mr Mitchell was having a pre-registration relax next morning when Doyle walked into the room. His eye was purple and swollen under his carefully-arranged blond hair. Mr Mitchell glanced at it, half-smiling.

'Oof!' he said. 'That's a beauty, Doyle! Who gave you that?'

Doyle stood still and gazed at him, completely self-contained.

'No one, sir. I hit it on a door at home.'

'I believe you,' said Mr Mitchell cheerily. 'Thousands wouldn't! Go and sit down.'

Doyle did so, amid an outbreak of deafening cheers.

'Right,' said Mr Mitchell. 'First things first. I'm sure you'll all be pleased to hear that the stolen flintlock has been returned. It arrived anonymously this morning. Miss Mather found it outside her room at half past eight.'

There were more cheers, lots more – real ones, now, not aimed at Michael Doyle.

'As a result,' said Mr Mitchell, 'the matter is now closed. The school festival will take place as scheduled.' He beamed. 'So I think we should all thank Ann Wilson for her suggestion of an amnesty.'

There was a chorus of congratulation. There was also a great big grin on Tucker's face, directed straight at Benny.

'Is this a private joke, Jenkins?' asked Mr Mitchell. 'Or can we all join in?'

'No sir,' said Tucker. 'It's just something that happened yesterday.'

'Ah,' said Mr Mitchell. 'I should have known, Jenkins. If you were involved it wouldn't be anything from which we could *all* benefit, would it?'

Tucker looked at Michael Doyle, and then at Benny once more. He laughed.

Ah, he thought. For once you could be wrong, sir.

It's possible.

CHAPTER NINE

Battles

Like a lot of bullies, Michael Doyle was always prepared to lower his sights a notch or two if it would make life easier. Having been beaten by the class, the teachers, and by Jenkins, he decided to go for what he saw as the weak link in the chain – Benny. Benny was only small, and he was easy going with it, unlike his best friend. As long as Doyle could do it craftily, so as not to fall foul of Tucker's anger – and his private army! – he thought he'd be all right. He set his mates up for the game as well; Robbo Robinson and Macker. They all had scores to settle.

Trisha Yates was spoiling for a fight these days, although she didn't exactly see it that way in her head. But she hadn't settled down at Grange Hill, really, despite the fact that everyone thought she was all right (everyone, that is except for Tucker Jenkins, who didn't count). She did not like school work, honestly, she found it boring and irrelevant. And lots of little things got up her nose. Every time she saw her sister, either ready to leave for school in the mornings, or queening it around the corridors with her dead-smart chums, Trisha seethed. She hated Carol, and she loved her. And she envied her to death – her clothes, her style, her make-up. It drove Trisha crazy with frustration.

Although she did not put it into words, Trisha was ripe for aggro. But no little, easy opponents for *her*. *She* was going to take on Grange Hill!

By coincidence, the first shot in Benny's war came seconds after he and Tucker had nearly knocked Trisha down in the playground – and got clouted with her briefcase for their pains. She had been walking out of school at teatime with Ann Wilson, and trying to persuade her to come down to the record shop.

'I've got homework,' said Ann. 'Haven't you?'

'Course I have,' said Trisha. 'You can do it after. Come on, don't be so boring.'

'No, I'd rather get it over,' said Ann. 'But that doesn't stop you going, does it?'

Oh yeah, thought Trisha. Great that would be, wouldn't it, going on her own? But before she could think of a pressing argument Tucker and Benny bombed them, and Ann was gone. She walked disconsolately homewards, her wrist hurting from the belt she'd given Tucker with her bag.

'Shall we go down the skating, Benno?' said Tucker.

'Can't,' said Ben. 'Me Dad's at hospital today and I've got to get home to mind our Michael.'

'How long's he going to be laid up, then? It's been ages.'

'Dunno,' Benny replied. 'Mum says he might not even get back ever. To work, like.'

'Flipping heck,' said Tucker. 'My Dad would do his nut if that happened to him. He went to work with a broken rib once. He didn't know he had it, like. Till the pain made him go to the doctor's and have it out.'

Benny fell about.

'You don't have ribs out, stupid. You have them fixed, like my Dad's back.'

'Yeah. Well, he had that done, didn't he? Hey! Alan! Hang about a bit!'

Alan Hargreaves and another boy had an old skateboard, and they all scooted off down the street on it, leaving Benny – fed up – to go home and do his duty. He turned away. Smack into Michael Doyle.

Michael Doyle grinned. He'd seen Tucker and Alan rolling out of sight. Doyle was not alone.

'Watch where you're going, Golliwog,' he said.

Benny despised racialists, because he knew they were short on brainpower. But that was no reason to ignore the insults.

'Who are you calling Golliwog?' he said. He made it sound aggressive, but three onto one with this lot was a hiding to nothing, let's face it.

'You,' said Doyle. 'Why? Think you can do something about it, do you? Now that Jenkins and Fatty Arbuckle aren't here to help you?'

113

David Robinson snatched the ball from Benny's hands. He dropped it onto his foot and booted it away down the street. They bunched tightly round him so that he could not run after it.

'Well, Golly?' said Robbo. 'What are you going to do about that?'

It was in Benny's mind to punch him in the gob, but he'd only end up slaughtered. Instead, he jumped suddenly at Macker. Who, taken by surprise, dropped back a foot. Benny, with a spurt of his famous football field acceleration, was through the gap and away.

They did not follow. They couldn't have caught him anyway. But they made ape noises at him, as he picked up the ball. With all the actions.

Trisha had her books spread out on the kitchen table, but she'd hardly looked at them when Carol came in and walked over to the mirror. She looked terrific, and Trisha had a painful stab of jealousy. But Carol's sweater was so good, she couldn't keep her stupid mouth shut.

'Coo,' she said. 'That's fantastic. Where d'you get it?'

'Never you mind. Just keep your paws off, that's all.'

'How much did it cost?'

Carol looked at herself smugly in the mirror, running a comb through her long brown hair.

'Nosey, aren't you?' she mocked.

Trisha got wild.

'You can be so childish at times!' she said. Carol put her tongue out.

'Listen who's talking then.'

Defeated, Trisha went back to 'doing' her homework. But Carol hadn't finished having fun.

'Still sulking are you, piglet? Because Mum wouldn't let you go to the rock concert?'

Resentment flared up anew.

'Yeah, she would if you'd take me, wouldn't she?'

Carol made a face of supercilious horror.

'You *must* be joking! Haven't you got a teddy bear you could play with instead?'

114

Trisha stuck her tongue out, then played a crafty card. She'd been keeping it in reserve.

'I'll tell Mum who you're going out with. Lucy Craven's brother.'

It struck home. Carol was shocked, then tried to hide it.

'How did you . . . So what, stupid?'

'You know you're not allowed to see him cause he's got a motorbike.'

Carol was now on thin ice. Trisha had the upper hand. Carol said uneasily: 'What she doesn't know won't hurt her, will it?'

'If you took me to the concert I wouldn't be *able* to tell Mum –'

Their mother had entered. She picked up the tail end of the sentence.

'Tell Mum what?'

Trisha left Carol on the hook. She wondered how best to play it to get what she wanted. She didn't dare just drop her in it, though. She had to be subtle.

'Er. Carol said she might take me to the rock concert, Mum.'

But Carol called her bluff.

'I did *not*' she said. And her mother cut straight in: 'You're not going *anywhere,* my girl.' With a dramatic gesture, she produced a pair of Trisha's multi-coloured tights. '*What* are these?'

Hell! She'd forgotten to take them out. She said accusingly: 'They were in my blazer pocket!'

'Yes,' said Mrs Yates. 'And what were they doing there, I'd like to know?'

'I . . . I took them in to show someone.'

Trisha looked dead guilty, which she was. They were not the ones she'd got detention for, from Miss Mather, but they were just as gaudy. She'd taken them to school to put on in the lavs, to show the girls, but she'd forgotten all about them. Her mother, reasonably enough, was unconvinced.

'Now listen, Trisha,' she said. 'I'm getting a little tired of all this nonsense. It's always something. If it isn't tights it's nail varnish. If it isn't –'

Trisha slammed her pencil down.

'Well, why can't I wear what I want to?' she demanded. 'Other girls my age do.'

'Because,' said Mrs Yates, 'the school *says* you can't.'

'*Why?*'

'Because it *does*! And I'm not going to stand here arguing about it! I never had any trouble from Carol and I'm not going to have any from you.'

Carol was laughing out loud. She was insufferable. For Trisha, it was either tears or sulkiness. And she was too angry to cry.

She muttered: 'It's not fair. *I* can never do anything.'

'No,' retorted her mother, in a calmer tone. 'Because you're in too much of a hurry to grow up for your own good, if you ask me. Before you know it you'll be in *real* trouble at that school.' She turned on a threatening note. 'And if you *do*, my girl.'

Carol, dolled up to the nines and raring to go, gave a 'tut-tut' grin to Trisha and opened the door to leave. Then she said provocatively: 'Bye, little sister. You be ever-so-ever-so good!'

Trisha snatched up a rubber and hurled it. It bounced across the kitchen.

'Temper temper!' said Carol.

'Trisha!' said Mum.

'It's not *fair*,' said Trisha Yates.

When Tucker Jenkins walked into the classroom next morning it was bedlam. Most of the boys and some of the girls were clustered in the front, roaring and shouting. In the narrow space between Mr Mitchell's desk and the front row there was a punch-up going on. He had to push his way through a lot of bodies before he could see who was fighting – Benny and Michael Doyle.

Benny was fighting hard, but he was easily getting the worst of it. When Tucker broke through, his head was poking out of Doyle's armpit and his face was being punched repeatedly. Everyone was shouting Benny on – much good that was doing him – but no one had joined in.

Tucker did. He launched himself into the fray, broke Doyle's headlock, and sent him sprawling. Then he picked his mate up off the floor.

Doyle sized up the situation, but did not start on Tucker. His memory was not that bad.

'Why don't you let him fight his own battles?' he said.

''Cause he's my mate and you're not,' returned Tucker. 'So push off. You all right Benny? What was it about?'

Tommy Watson said: 'He was giving him aggro about wearing jeans and that.'

'So why didn't you help him out, Crumbo?'

'Oh,' said Watson. 'Well, I was just going to but you –'

'Yah,' said Tucker, in disgust.

'Good morning!' said the cheery voice of Mr Mitchell. 'What's going on? This place is like a bear garden! Sit down, all of you.'

Trisha Yates came to with a jerk. She'd been a thousand miles away throughout the brawl. She'd been dealing with much much more important matters. Now she desperately tried to get the top screwed on the nail varnish bottle and put it in her desk before Old Mitchell noticed. And without smudging the shiny brown.

It was the smell that gave her away, probably. The heady smell of acetone she loved so much. Mr Mitchell stood above her while the rest of the class looked on. Dozy Yates was at it again . . .

'Hands.'

Trisha showed them, palms up. Mr Mitchell waited until she gave in and turned them over.

'See me afterwards,' he said.

The scene at the end of the lesson was short and not too sweet. In fact it was the bitterest experience Trisha Yates had ever had in her few short weeks at Grange Hill. Because she'd finally got right up Mr Mitchell's nose. Out of sight. His voice was vibrant with suppressed anger. He actually sounded as if he disliked her. To her surprise, Trisha found that that hurt. It hurt her very much indeed.

'Well,' he said, without bothering to leave his desk. 'What have you got to say for yourself?' No reply. 'Come here!'

Trisha stood before him, a defiant expression on her face.

'And stop degrading yourself by behaving like a playground lout,' he said. 'We have more than enough of the real thing already. Besides which it displays a degree of stupidity which I know you don't possess. So what's it all about?'

Trisha wanted to respond, to win back some approval. But it wouldn't happen right.

'What's what about?' she said sullenly.

'All right,' said Mr Mitchell. 'If you want to play games.' He spoke to her like a four-year-old: 'Why . . . are . . . you . . . wearing . . . nail . . . varnish?'

'Dunno.'

He breathed evenly for a time.

'And what does the school rule say?'

'Can't wear it.'

'And how many times have you been told?'

'Dunno.'

'Then *why* are you wearing it?'

Trisha did not have an answer. What answer could there be? She shrugged.

'Perhaps you are stupid, after all,' said Mr Mitchell quietly.

Suddenly, Trisha flared up.

'It's not *me* that's stupid, it's this school that's stupid,' she almost yelled. 'I can't see what's wrong with wearing what you want!'

The teacher got riled as well.

'*Can't* you?' he snapped. 'Well, it's not up to you to decide, is it?'

'It's me that has to wear the stupid uniform!'

Trisha was staring at him rudely. Mr Mitchell gripped the sides of his desk.

'I'm . . . I'm not going to argue with you, Trisha. My job is only –'

'*Yes*! That's all anyone ever says!'

She'd gone too far.

'Right!' said Mr Mitchell. 'I can see I'm not going to get anywhere with you. Perhaps I might get somewhere with your parents.'

The shock got her in the stomach.

'What do you mean?' she said. Her voice had changed, but Mr Mitchell's remained raised.

'I'll write them a letter to come and see me,' he said. 'That might –'

'Oh please, sir! Don't do that, sir! I'm sorry I argued. I won't do it again, sir. *Honestly.*'

'And how many times, Trisha, have I heard *that* before?'

She said humbly: 'I really *mean* it this time, sir.'

Mr Mitchell swept his papers off his desk and turned for the door.

'No, I'm sorry,' he said. 'This time we're going to sort it out. *Once* and for all!'

He even slammed the door behind him.

Trisha slept badly that night, with worrying. Her mother had given her warning after warning, just like Mr Mitchell. She did not know what the punishment would be, but it would be something horrible, certainly. Her father would be brought in as well, probably. And Carol, rotten Carol, would have a ball. She was tired in the morning, and felt a little odd. Funny, light-headed, jumpy. She didn't know what to do.

Carol came down in a sunny mood, and didn't even shout at her for using all the breakfast milk. She went out to the step to get some more, which gave Trisha the beginnings of a daft idea. A *really* daft idea.

'Has the postman been?' she asked.

'Oh – it talks, does it?' said Carol, putting the milk bottle on the table. 'Why? Expecting a letter, are you?'

'No,' said Trisha. 'A sack of coal, stupid. *Has* he?'

At that instant, the letterbox gave a rattle. Carol chuckled.

'There's the coalman!'

There were four letters on the mat, and Trisha flicked through them hurriedly. There was one with the Grange Hill crest. She heard her mother close a bedroom door. And almost without thinking, she stuffed the letter into her blazer pocket. Then Mrs Yates came trotting down the stairs.

'Anything exciting?' she asked, holding her hand out. She glanced at the envelopes. 'Bills,' she sighed. 'That's all we ever seem to get.'

Trisha was jumpy.

'I'm going now,' she said.

Her mother looked at her sternly.

'Just a minute, my girl. What have you got in those pockets?'

Trisha was flabbergasted. She gabbled: 'What . . . what d'you mean?'

'No fancy stockings, I hope? No earrings?'

Oh, the relief!

'No, Mum. Honest.'

'Well,' said Mrs Yates. 'Just keep it that way, eh?'

'Yes, Mum. OK. Bye.'

She had escaped . . .

The enormity of what she had done weighed more and more heavily on Trisha as she got closer to Grange Hill. It was absurd, ridiculous, to think she could get away with it. What would happen when Mr Mitchell didn't get a reply? Would he think the fairies had got it? Would he think the cat had eaten it? Would he reckon Trisha's parents just weren't bothering? Would he hell. And all the trouble that had been coming would be doubled, trebled, millionled. What *had* she done?

Near the gates, Trisha stopped altogether, and took the letter out. Should she take it home and drop it through the letterbox? Should she throw herself under a bus? Should she . . .? The letter blurred under her gaze and she stuffed it back into her pocket. Without knowing why, and without knowing where, she turned and walked away. Then she was running.

Benny Green lay in the caretaker's basement junk room and read a football mag while he waited for Tucker to appear. When he heard footsteps on the stairs he did not turn round – they had a rendezvous. Before he realized his mistake it was too late. He was trapped.

Michael Doyle reached over Benny's shoulder and

snatched the magazine. He tore a page out and threw it to the floor.

'We've got some unfinished business to settle, haven't we?'

Benny did not try to get up from the bench he was sprawled on, because he knew he wouldn't make it. Robbo and Macker were hovering just behind their boss.

'You might, Doyle,' he replied. 'I haven't.'

'You know what my Dad says about this lot?' said Doyle to his friends. 'He says they should all be sent back where they belong.'

'Yeah!' said Macker. 'In the jungle!'

Benny twisted his neck round to see Doyle more clearly.

'Your Dad should be where he belongs, then,' he said. 'In a loony bin.'

Doyle rolled the magazine up tightly and began hitting Benny over the head with it.

'Don't you say things like that about my Dad,' he snarled.

'*His* Dad's on the council,' said Robbo.

Macker added: '*He's* not on the dole.'

They were all poking and punching at him now. There was no way Benny could get out of it.

Doyle said: 'That's where you got your jacket, isn't it? Off the dole.'

'My Mum got it for me.'

'Yeah, off the Social Security,' sneered Macker.

'So what?' said Benny, desperately. The more he could keep them talking the more chance he had of Tucker turning up. 'We can't help it if my Dad's sick.'

'That's why you can't afford any trousers, I suppose,' said Robbo.

'What's it to do with you?' He tried to sit up, but Robbo shoved him flat onto the bench.

'If *we've* got to wear proper uniforms,' said Doyle. 'So should you.'

'Hey!' said Macker. Brainwave. 'If he's not going to wear trousers – he shouldn't be allowed to wear jeans!'

Doyle got the message.

'Right!' he cried. 'Come on, lads! Let's have them off him.'

Benny struggled and kicked but the odds were impossible. He was pushed off the bench onto the floor and Doyle kept smacking at his face while the others tore at his shoe laces and his belt.

'Come on, Golly,' Doyle shouted, as Benny tried to land a punch. 'You can do better than that!'

They had not got very far – one shoe off and his belt undone – when the registration bell rang. Trust Tucker to be late today of all days. The three boys ran off, making grunting noises and lolloping like chimpanzees. At the top of the stairs, Robbo turned and chucked his shoe back, bouncing it off his chest. Benny was alone.

He felt terrible. He wasn't hurt but he was very close to crying. Two dimbos and a rotten little bully whose Dad was on the council. And they could put him into this state. It was wrong. It was stupid. It was mad. Why did they want to pick on him?

Benny had got his trainer back on when Tucker scuttled down the stairs. He picked up the remains of the football magazine.

'Aye-aye,' he said. 'What's been going on?'

'Nothing,' mumbled Benny. Going over it all again with Tucker wasn't going to help, was it? He'd help him bash up Doyle, maybe. But what was the good of that?

'Who did this, then?'

'No one,' said Benny. He pushed past Tucker and ran up the steps. He wouldn't look at him. Outside Tucker seized him by the arm.

'Hang on, Benny! What's the problem?'

But Benny pulled away. He started to stomp off, his ball clamped under his left arm. *Away* from their classroom.

'Where are you going?' asked Tucker. Benny carried on. Tucker shouted. 'Hey, Dimhead! Benny! It's registration!'

As Benny went out of sight around a corner, Mr Mitchell came on Tucker, who was standing looking stupid.

'Come on, man,' he said. 'You're late.'

Mr Mitchell did not discover until after lunch that Trisha Yates was playing truant – and then he found out only by accident. He had no idea at all that Benny was, because Tucker was the only one who knew, and he wasn't saying anything.

The discovery about Trisha came about because Mr Mitchell had asked Ann Wilson, who went the same way home, to pop in on Trisha's at lunchtime. She had – and it had been very embarrassing. Because it quickly became apparent that Mrs Yates thought Trisha was at school, and having dinner there, as she sometimes liked to do. Ann had had to pretend that *she'd* been ill, so had not seen Trisha. Ridiculous.

'But you can't be *sure* she's playing truant,' said Mary when Ann told her just before afternoon school. They were alone in the classroom, sorting out their things.

'What *else* can she be doing?' Ann replied. 'If her own *mother* thinks she's at school she *must* be playing truant.'

'Are you going to tell Mr Mitchell?' asked Mary. And behind them both, the teacher walked quietly into the room.

'I don't know,' said Ann. 'Do you think I should?'

'Well,' said Mary, doubtfully. 'You'll have to tell him something. Old Mitch is bound to ask, isn't he?'

Said Mr Mitchell: 'And what *exactly* is "Old Mitch" bound to ask?'

So that was that. Fifteen minutes later, having settled with Miss Mather that she'd guard his class until he got back, he set off to find his wandering girl. Miss Mather – who'd had a free period and now did not – said mildly: 'It's not your job to search for truants, surely?'

'No, June,' he said. 'But I think this is my fault. This girl was wearing nail varnish and I – I lost my temper and fired a letter off to her parents.'

'Ah,' said June Mather. 'It wouldn't be Trisha Yates by any chance?'

'Of course,' said Mr Mitchell. 'Who else? But she's a good kid really. And as I started it, I suppose I'd like to finish it. That's all.'

Miss Mather smiled.

'Where are you going to look?'

He gestured at the window. It was spitting with rain.

'Judging by the weather, she'll be indoors somewhere. If she's got any sense.'

'Ah. The Civic Centre's your best bet, then.'

'Why?'

She raised her eyebrows.

'Because it's close,' she said. 'And *free*.'

'Ah,' said Mr Mitchell. 'Cleverclogs!'

Cleverclogs or not, Miss Mather was right. Trisha Yates was in the Civic Centre library, and she was doing something she wouldn't normally have done for a thousand pounds. She was visiting an art show.

It was in a big, light airy room on the first floor, and Trisha had been there since dinnertime. Dinner had been a hamburger and a Mars bar, because luckily she was flush. So she wasn't hungry, and she wasn't frightened any more. She'd had a bad moment going in, and had worked out some story about the art exhibition being part of a school project she had to do. But nobody had even bothered to speak to her. She wasn't hungry and she wasn't frightened – she was bored. She'd walked miles, looked in shops, got wet in a shower. And she was wild with boredom. To think some people truanted for fun!

Benny Green was bored as well, but he was hungry too. Benny was not flush today or any day. He had precisely nothing. His cover story had been that the school had a half day or something, but no one had asked him either. Because like Trisha, Benny had ended up where it was dry and warm. At the other end of the big, light gallery – he was getting culture as well! Ruddy hell, he thought, for the umpteenth time. What do people see in pictures . . .

The way they ran into each other was like something out of the cartoons. There were upright screens everywhere, on little legs, with posters and suchlike stuck to them. They both backed round one in the end, their minds in neutral and their eyes glazed with the tediousness of it all. They were practically blind. And they bumped right into each other. Trisha turned.

'Oh, sorry,' she began. Then: 'Benny!'

They smiled sheepishly, pleased, for the first time ever, to see each other.

'Blimey,' she said. 'Have you bunked off as well? It's dead *boring*, isn't it?'

There were big soft plastic couches all around, so they went and flopped on one. Benny said after a while: 'What did you bunk off for?'

'I wish I knew,' said Trisha. She pulled the crumpled envelope from her pocket. 'Old Mitch sent this to my Mum and Dad. So I goes and intercepts it, don't I! Not realizing he'll want an answer. When I got to school I just sort of panicked and ran off. I've been worrying about it ever since. I mean they're going to find out, aren't they? They're bound to.'

'I suppose so. What's the letter all about?'

'About me wearing nail varnish and stuff. You know.' She shrugged. 'Stupid, innit? What you doing here?'

Benny looked away.

'No come on, Benny,' Trisha said. 'I told *you*. What's up with you? Look, I'm not going to *tell* anyone, am I?'

'Well,' he said. 'It's that Mickey Doyle.'

Trisha pulled a face.

'Ooergh! Him!'

Benny nodded. At least she seemed to hate him, too.

'He keeps going on about me not having a proper uniform and that.'

'Well, that's not your fault, is it? Your Dad's on the sick.' She flicked her skirt with her fingernail. 'I wish I could wear jeans to school instead of this stupid thing, anyway.'

'It's different when you have to, though,' he said. He decided to go the whole hog. 'He keeps on calling me names, too.'

'What sort of names? Go on, it helps you sometimes if you tell, honest it does.'

Benny looked down.

'Just the usual. Golliwog. Chocolate. And the chimpanzee noises and that.'

'Ooh I can't stand him,' said Trisha. 'He's *horr*ible.' Then she decided to make a joke, to show him she really cared. 'Anyway,' she said. 'It's not your fault you're a nignog, is it!'

It wasn't the first time for Benny and it wouldn't be the last, but he still hated it. Still, he knew Trisha meant well, she was trying to break the ice. She was nice, in fact; it was amazing. If he ever got to know her better, he could explain it properly. For now, he countered with a joke of his own.

'It's not your fault you're a honky, either!' he said. And Trisha, grinning, gave him a friendly push.

They were talking about Tucker when Mr Mitchell found them, with Benny trying to convince Trisha that he was actually a nice bloke. Trisha, although she'd taken to Benny quite a lot since they'd met in such peculiar circumstances, wasn't having *that*, though. Halfway through the argument, they heard a voice they recognized. It was Mr Mitchell talking to the attendant. About a girl with long blonde hair . . .

Benny and Trisha tried to hide, but they had no chance. Apart from anything else, their feet showed underneath the screens. Mr Mitchell cornered them. Seeing Benny as well as Trisha came as rather a shock, of course. But he hid it well. He led them to a couch and they all perched down.

'Well,' he said. 'Who's going to start? What about you, Trisha? I think I know why *you're* here. The letter?' Trisha, nodding, fished it from her pocket. She handed it to him silently. 'And do you think running away has solved anything?'

'Probably made it worse, sir,' she said.

'And all because you wouldn't obey a few simple rules.' Trisha was beyond arguing. Or temper.

'But why do I *have* to, sir?'

Mr Mitchell tried to look like a wise old uncle, although he didn't exactly fill the part.

'It's a question of discipline, Trisha,' he said. 'The school has a uniform, so you must –'

'But *other* schools don't have them!'

'No,' he said. 'But we, Trisha, do. Some people, you see, think to have a uniform instils a sense of belonging, it makes everyone equal. *You* should understand that, Benny, being a member of the football team, all wearing the same strip.'

That's a laugh, thought Trisha.

'Yeah,' she said. 'It's all right if everyone's *given* a uniform, sir, but otherwise it doesn't work. Look at Benny – *he's* being made to suffer because everyone knows his parents can't *afford* a proper one.'

'Is that why you're here, Benny?' asked Mr Mitchell.

'More or less, sir,' mumbled Benny. He didn't reckon much on all this heavy talk.

Trisha blurted out: 'That Doyle's been picking on him, sir. Because of his uniform and his Dad being sick and . . . and him being coloured, sir.'

Mr Mitchell looked dead thoughtful.

'Ah,' he went. There was silence for quite some little while. Then he sighed. 'Look,' he said. 'I wish I could offer you some simple answers – but I can't. It seems to me . . . Look, to some extent you're both suffering from the same problem – you both feel you're being picked on. You, Benny, by Doyle and his friends, and you, Trisha, by the school. Right?'

Fair enough. They nodded.

'Now you, Benny,' went on Mr Mitchell. 'Are being singled out because through circumstances, you *are* different. Whereas with you, Trisha, it's for *wanting* to be. And of the two of you, I'd say Benny has the greater problem, wouldn't you. Because Benny has no choice in the matter – but you, young lady, have.'

She looked at him, then Benny. It sounded like good sense.

'And if you disagree with the uniform *so* much,' said Mr Mitchell. 'Why not do the thing properly and join the existing campaign for its abolition?'

Trisha grinned. She had an answer to *that*, at least!

'Yeah,' she said. 'But what's Benny going to do?'

Mr Mitchell acknowledged the joke, but stayed serious.

'That's very much up to him,' he said. 'You're always going to run into people like Doyle, Benny, but hopefully they'll be far outnumbered by people ready to accept you for yourself. And Doyle, for example – is *not* in the football team, now is he?'

'No chance,' said Benny. 'He's crap, that kid. In every way. I'll be all right, sir. Don't you worry. Sorry about the swearing.'

'I didn't hear a word,' smiled Mr Mitchell. He looked at both their faces, wondering how much of it had sunk in. You're good kids, he thought. I really like you both. It was time to make a gesture.

'Now look you two,' he said briskly. 'You shouldn't really have done this.' With rapid movements he tore the letter into four pieces and stuffed them into his pocket. He grinned, suddenly. 'But we'll say no more about it!'

Trisha's face was a picture. Benny almost laughed. When Mr Mitchell got onto his feet, they followed suit.

'*Providing*,' the teacher added, 'you are back in school tomorrow. *Both* of you. *And* with smiling faces. Well? Is it a deal?'

It sounded fine. To both of them. It was a deal.

After all, they agreed, when Mr Mitchell had left them alone among the pictures once again – *anything* was better than boredom!

Next morning they *were* both back – although Trisha did manage to turn up late. At first things felt slightly different, for both of them: they looked at Mr Mitchell with new eyes. But five minutes after registration, work was in full swing.

And Tucker had managed to give Trisha a crafty smack without being seen by sir.

And Trisha had got him back, a good one.

And Doyle had glowered secretly at Benny Green: I'll get you, chum.

And Benny had responded with contempt. Just you try it.

They were back to the grindstone, noses down, the unpaid wageslaves of Grange Hill – with the future just about to happen.

It was business as usual . . .